FOLKTALES FROM AROUND THE WORLD

Volume One

Author Norma Jean

Illustrated by Illana Miller

Edited by Sally Braun-Jackson

Folktales from around the world

COPYRIGHT 2011 BY Norma Gangaram

Printed in Canada

Publisher Norma Gangaram

Registration Number

ISBN 978-0-9867032-6-3

Dedicated to My Grandchildren

Taylor and Nicholas

This book belong to _____

Date   _____

If you borrowed this book and you enjoyed it, I invite you to purchase your own copy at http://www.childrensstories.ca

Table of Contents

I take no credit for any of the stories in this book they have been retold for the enjoyment of my grand children and the young readers in my family.

THE BRAVE LITTLE PARROT

An ancient folktale from Jataka, India Retold.

There once was a parrot that enjoyed living in her natural habitat of the forest. Amidst her contentment, a storm struck that would change her life forever. As the storm struck, it was accompanied by lightning and thunder. To the parrot's amazement, the lighting hit a dry dead tree, and it burst into flames. As the flames rose, the embers flew into the skies. In her fear and anxiety, the parrot kept the tree moving to avoid being burnt.

With the strong smell of smoke in the air, the parrot raised the alarm by shouting, "Fire! Run for the river," and with that she spread her wings and flew to the safety of the water. She was very grateful that she could fly and would escape imminent danger. While in flight, she looked down on the land and saw many animals in danger of being burnt since they were caught in the middle of the raging fire. In desperation, the parrot started to think about what she could do to help the situation.

Suddenly, she got a bright idea which might help her friends. She flew over the water and saturated herself with it, and then she doubled back over the raging fire. The heavy smoke clouded her vision and burned her eyes, impairing her vision, but she pressed onward despite having to dodge the rising embers. When the little parrot got to the rising flames, she shook the water off her wing feathers. Miraculously, the droplets of water sprinkled like smouldering gems onto the flames below and extinguished them.

Many times, the little parrot flew back and forth between the river and the burning forest, each time saturating herself with water and sprinkling the water on the angry flames. Each trip to the river brought success as the flames began to quiet down.

The little parrot repeated this behaviour several times in an effort to save her forest friends. The high intensity of the fire's heat burnt her feathers. Her feet and claws were seared. Her lungs ached from the acrid stench and her eyes smarted from the smoke. She was in danger of becoming disorientated, but she would not give up. Still, the little parrot pressed on with determination to save her friends.

In a moment of terror, some of the blissful gods afloat high overhead in their cloud homes of ivory and gold looked down and saw the little parrot flying back and forth among the flames. As they sat at their luxurious dining table, between mouthfuls of honeyed foods, they shouted gleefully, "Look at that silly bird! She's trying to do the impossible by putting out a raging forest fire with a few sprinkles of water!" As they laughed, they thought, "How could anyone be so illogical?"

Despite all the laughter, one of the gods, oddly moved, took the form of a golden eagle and flew down to the busy little parrot. As the parrot once more approached the flames, the eagle, with eyes like molten gold became visible at her side.

"Stop, little bird!" said the eagle in a solemn and majestic tone. "Your insignificant trips back and forth are hopeless. A few drops of water won't smoulder a forest fire. Give it up, and save yourself before it is too late."

The little parrot ignored the majestic eagle and continued to fly through the smoke and flames. As she worked, she could hear the great eagle flying above her. As the heat grew in its intensity, the eagle called out, "Stop, foolish little parrot! It is useless! Save yourself!"

The parrot replied angrily, "I don't need some majestic, shining eagle to tell me what I already know. My own mother, the dear bird, could have given me this lesson long ago. I don't need any advice. I just need someone to help!" She coughed as she flew through the smoke.

As we know, the eagle was a god. He watched the parrot endeavouring to put out the flames. High above him, he could see his own kind – those happy-go-lucky gods – being entertained by the parrot's sincere effort to cause a change, even as many animals cried out in pain and fear far below. The eagle felt embarrassed for the gods who were enjoying a carefree life. A new burning desire grew in his heart.

The eagle thought, "Even though I am a god, I wish I could be just like the little parrot that flies alone with great determination, risking everything to help her friends. What a noble creature! What a great little parrot!" Stimulated by these desires, the great eagle began to shed tears. A flood of sparkling tears fell from his eyes. Then, streams of tears fell, washing down like showers of rain upon the fire, the forest, the animals and the little parrot, too.

As the heavenly tears fell, the raging fire slowed and eventually died. Smoke continued to rise up from the smouldering earth; yet, new life was already boldly shooting forth stems, blossoms and leaves. Even green grass started to come to life among the still-hot cinders.

A heavenly teardrop from the eagle shone on the little parrot's wings. New feathers started to grow: Red, green, yellow and every colour of the rainbow. Magnificent colors! She became a very pretty bird, indeed.

The animals looked at each other in awe. They were transformed. Everyone was saved from peril. Up above in the clear blue sky, everyone could see their brave little parrot, determined to cause a change even at the expense of her own life. Her love had her soaring in delight. When all hope was gone, somehow she had saved them.

"Bravo!" they cried. "Bravo, for our brave little parrot and for this sudden, miraculous rain!"

JIU-ROKU-ZAKURA

A Japanese folktale Version One Retold

In Japan, in the district of Wakegori of the province of Iyo, it is said that there is a very old cherry tree that is very famous. It is called Jiu-roku-zakura, or "The Cherry tree of the Sixteenth Day." It has this name because this tree only blooms every year on the sixteenth day of the first month, as measured by the old lunar calendar. On the sixteenth day of the first month, the cherry tree will present its villagers with her beautiful blooms despite the cold weather of the season. In the real world, the cherry tree naturally tends to wait for the spring season before showing the world its beautiful blossoms. The people of Wakegori believe that the Jiu-roku-zakura blossoms possess a supernatural power. They believe the ghost of a man lives in the tree, and that it is because of him that this unnatural phenomenon occurs every winter.

The ghost of the man who lives in the cherry tree is believed to be a samurai from Iyo. The tree grew in his garden and bloomed every year in the spring, just like all the other trees. As a child, he loved that tree and would play under it. For many generations, the man's family members had admired the tree's blossoms. The tree was thought to be one hundred years old, and over the years, many people had written poems, expressing praise and gratitude, on brightly coloured papers, which were hung on its branches as decorations.

As one might expect, the young boy grew into a man, and finally became an old man. All of his life, he adored the cherry tree because it held so many precious memories for him. The man had such a long life that he outlived his family. All that was left of his life was the cherry tree. Unfortunately, in the summer of the year, the tree withered and died.

The old man was heartbroken! He mourned the tree and everything it had meant for himself and his ancestors. The neighbours, seeing the old man's pain, decided to plant another young, beautiful cherry tree to take the place of the old one in the garden. They hoped the new tree would bring comfort and delight to the old man. He was grateful and thanked his neighbours, and he pretended to be delighted with his new cherry tree. However, his heart was breaking. He remembered spending so many years of his childhood playing under the tree, but he had loved that tree so much that there was nothing that could have consoled him for its loss.

Then one day he had a light-bulb moment, a most cheerful thought: he had come up with a way that the dying tree might be rescued. As it happened, this day was the sixteenth day of the first month. The man walked into his garden and humbly bowed before the withered tree. He spoke to it, saying: "Now, deign, I beseech you, once more to bloom, because I am going to die in your place." The people of Iyo believed that one could die in the place of another and by doing so, with the blessing of the gods, sacrifice one's life for the benefit of another, a practice expressed by the term *migawari ni tatsu*, or to "act as a substitute." Then, the man carefully spread a white sheet under the tree, sat down upon the coverings, and carried out *hara-kiri* as a samurai would do. Thus, it is said that the ghost of the old man now abides in the tree and makes it blossom on that same day and hour every year.

So it is said every year that the tree still blooms on the sixteenth day of the first month, in the season of winter.

JIU-ROKU-ZAKURA, THE CHERRY-TREE

A Japanese folktale Version two- Retold

In Japan, in the province of Iyo, there is a district called Wakegori. According to folklore, this story was supposed to have taken place there. In this district, there is a very famous old cherry tree, and it is known as Jiu-roku-zakura, or "the Cherry-tree of the Sixteenth Day." The reason for this name being given to this tree is because this tree only blossoms every year on the sixteenth day of the first month. It is not January since the months at that time were measured by the old lunar calendar. Only on that day will the blooms bless the natives with their flowery beauty. What is so unusual about this story is the time of the bloom is in the winter which as we all know is cold, a time when everything lays dormant.

Under normal circumstances, the natural tendencies of a cherry-tree would be to wait for the spring time before manifesting to the world it beautiful flowers. The natives of the province of Iyo in the district of Wakegori are of the belief that the Jiu-roku-zakura blossoms hold within it a life that has a mystical power; at least that is what the natives have been told. They hold onto the belief that it is the spirit of a man who resides in that tree. They are of the opinion that he causes this going against nature occurrence to take place every single winter.

The people are of the opinion that this spirit is that of a samurai of Iyo; they believe that the tree grew in his garden as a child and was a normal tree which blossoms in the spring time like all other trees; blooming time being just about the end of March or the beginning of April. As a child, the samurai adored that tree and enjoyed many hours of play under the shade of this tree. This tree has been there for many generations of grandparents and his parents. These blossoms would grace this tree with it presence every season for more than a hundred years enjoyed by all. The natives are so passionate about this tree that they have taken time to write poems of praise and gratitude on brightly coloured paper hung as decorations on this tree.

However, that young boy grew and became a man, but he never out-grew his love for the tree. His adoration was because the tree held many precious memories for generations. He was blessed with a long life, out-living his own family. Even as an old man, he still found solace under that tree. In his world, the only thing of beauty left for him that held so many memories was the old cherry tree. Then one summer, the tree withered and died!

The old man was heartbroken once again by yet another loss, his tree, and grieved the numerous memories of many lives. The neighbours felt the pain of the old man and decided to plant another beautiful cherry-tree for him. They hoped it would fill the void in the old man's heart. They hoped the young tree would bring some comfort to the old man.

He was very grateful and thanked his friends, and made everyone believe that he was delighted with his young cherry tree. None the less, his heart ached for his old tree. He loved the old tree so very much because it held a life time of memories that had enriched his life. He was quietly inconsolable.

There are several versions of this folktale: another tells the story that, in fact, in his depression, the old samurai committed suicide under the tree.

WILLOW WIFE

Japanese folktale Retold

In Japan, there is a very famous village; and in this village, there is a certain great willow tree much loved by many generations for hundreds of years. Because of its welcoming branches which droop like nature's umbrella, in the summer it was a resting place from a hot summer's day. It was also a meeting place where the villagers would congregate after work and the heat of the day were over. This tree was so welcoming that the villagers would sit and chat until the moonlight started to peek through the branches. In winter, it was like a snow covered umbrella with sparkling snow gleaming in the sun.

A young farmer by the name of Heitaro lived very close to this tree. He had come to love this willow very much. It was a part of his life and had a lot of childhood memories of playing under this tree with him. Heitaro had a special relationship with the willow: beneath her branches he spent a lot of time in

contemplation. He worked out many of his problems there, and she held a special place in his heart.

Upon rising in the morning, Heitaro would see the happy willow tree swaying in the gentle breeze welcoming the new day. As he made his way home, he looked for his beloved willow with her branches beckoning him home. Heitaro cherished this willow so very much that sometimes he took the time to burn a joss-stick under her branches and kneel down in prayerful communion with his god. This willow heard all his prayers, his deepest secrets, his concerns, his gratitude and his love as he would pray to his god.

Then one day a fellow villager came to Heitaro and told him that the villagers were thinking of building a bridge over the river. They wished to have the great willow tree for timber.

"For timber?" said Heitaro, hiding the distress of his face in his hands. "My dear willow tree for timber to build a bridge, only to have everyone constantly using her to walk upon and all she will hear all day was the thumping of feet! No never, never, old man!"

After Heitaro had gotten over the original shock of the news, and as he came back to reality, he offered to donate some of his own trees, if the villagers would accept them for timber and save the ancient willow.

The villagers willingly accepted this offer, and the willow tree was spared. It continued to serve as a land mark for its people.

Then one night as Heitaro sat under the great willow, he suddenly saw a beautiful woman standing close beside him, looking at him timidly, as if she had something to say but did not know quite how to say it.

"Beautiful lady," said he, "Am I interrupting a planned meeting? I will be happy to leave. It seems as though you are waiting for a companion." Heitaro was very kind, respectful and polite to everyone.

"Oh, I do not think he will come," said the woman with a gentle smile.

"Could he have decided not to come, or has he changed his mind? Maybe he got cold feet!" suggested Heitaro.

"He has not gotten cold feet, my dear lord."

"Then, why does he not come? What strange occurrence is this?"

"Oh, he has come alright! His heart has always been here under this willow tree." And on that note, she gave him a radiant smile, and then she vanished.

Each and every time they got together under the old willow tree, the beautiful woman's bashfulness totally disappeared, and it seemed that she could not hear enough from Heitaro's lips about his praises of the willow under which they sat.

Then one night he could not stand to be without his love any longer. He asked her, "Beautiful lady, will you be my wife, you my lady who seem to belong to the very tree itself?"

"Yes," replied the woman. "My name is Higo. Call me Higo (Willow) and moreover, you do not need to ask anyone for my hand in marriage. I have no father or mother. However, one day it will all make sense to you."

Heitaro and Higo were married, and before long they were blessed with a child, whom they called Chiyodo. Even though, their home was a very humble dwelling, the couple that lived there was the happiest family in all of Japan.

Then one day there was cause for celebration. Everyone in the village was talking about it. Heitaro and his family went about their daily duties not knowing there was going to be a celebration, but the good news was everywhere and so it was not long before the news reached Heitaro's ears.

The Emperor Toba had declared the desire to build a temple in Kyoto to Kwannon, the goddess of mercy. There was a great need for timber. Influential bureaucrats sent messages far and wide in search of timber. The villagers were moved by the request and wanted very much to contribute toward the building of the sacred structure by donating their ancient willow tree.

Heitaro could not persuade them to donate other trees. Only Heitaro could give such a large and handsome tree as the great willow tree.

Upon arriving at home, Heitaro shared his sad news with his wife. "Oh, my beautiful wife, the villagers will be cutting down our treasured willow tree! Before I married you, I could not bear to lose this tree. Having you, my dear, will perhaps help me get over losing my tree. You fill my heart."

That night, Heitaro was awakened by a most mournful and painful cry. He called out to his wife, "It is very dark! The room is full of soft voices. Are you there?"

Then his wife replied, "Heitaro, listen! They are taking down the willow tree. Look how it is shaking and trembling in the moonlight. I am the soul of the willow tree and the villagers are slaughtering me. Look at how they are cutting and tearing me to pieces! Dear Heitaro, the grief, the pain! Put your hands here and feel my heart breaking in anguish."

"My beautiful Willow wife! My beautiful Willow wife!" cried Heitaro.

"My dear husband," said Higo, very softly, cuddling her wet, tormented face close to his. "I am leaving you now. Please know that a love such as ours cannot be destroyed however hurtful the blows are. I shall wait for you and Chiyodo. My branches are falling from the sky! My body is breaking!"

Just at that moment there came a loud bang outside. The great willow tree lay on the ground powerless and green and slain mercilessly. Heitaro looked around for his beautiful wife, the one he loved more than anything else in the world.

His Willow Wife was gone! She was taken from him.

WHY THE EVERGREEN TREES KEEP THEIR LEAVES

IN WINTER

One day, a long, long time ago, as the winter was quickly approaching, and all the birds knew it was time to start their flight south to warmer countries, one little bird with a broken wing knew he could not make the long flight. He felt at a disadvantage because he knew he would need a home for the winter. He looked all round to see if there was any tree that would host him for the long winter and would give him warmth over the long winter. Finally, he spotted the trees in the enormous forest.

As he looked upon the trees he wondered, "Just maybe one of these trees will oblige me with some warm shelter over the long cold the winter."The wounded bird managed to get to the edge of the forest, leaping and quivering with the help of his damaged wing. As he leaped to the first tree, he saw that it was a slim silver birch. He asked politely, "Lofty birch-tree, would you be kind enough to let me abide in your warm branches through the winter until springtime comes?" "Oh my dearest!" moaned the birch-tree in reply."What a strange request! I have to nurture my own leaves through the winter; that is more than enough for me to handle. No, I am sorry."The little bird, feeling rejected leaped and quivered in pain from the broken wing until he arrived at the next tree. It was a giant, oak-tree.

"Oh towering oak-tree," cried the trembling little bird, "would you be kind

enough to let me abide in your warm branches through the winter until springtime comes?" "Oh my dearest," stuttered the oak-tree, "what a strange request! I am sorry I cannot grant you your request; I am sorry your request is an imposition to me! If you live in my branches through the winter you will be consuming my acorns. No, I am sorry."So the little bird leaped and quivered with his broken wing until he arrived at willow-tree by the edge of the stream.

"Oh huge willow-tree, would you be kind enough to let me abide in your warm branches through the winter until springtime comes?" cried the little bird. "No, not ever," yelled the willow-tree. "I do not know you! You are a stranger. Be gone!"

The poor little bird was beginning to become quite desperate and feared he would perish. He did not know who to turn to for help; however, he leaped and quivered, struggling with his broken wing. Then suddenly he was noticed by the spruce-tree, who asked, "What are you up to, gentle, little bird? You should have gone south." "I do not know what I am up to. No one will tolerate my presence in their branches for the long winter until spring arrives. You see my wing is broken, and I cannot fly, kind sir," sobbed the broken little bird.

"Why, I would be happy to have you stay on my branches," giggled the spruce. "Here, I will show you the warmest place of all."

"Thank you!" replied the bird. "You do know I need to stay all winter?"

"Yes," chuckled the spruce. "I would love to have your company all winter just to hear you sing for me."

The pine tree that was standing next to the spruce took pity on the little bird when he saw the little bird leaping and quivering with his broken wing. In a kind, warm voice, the pine tree murmured, "My branches will not give you much warmth, but I can keep the wind at bay since I am big and strong."

Feeling unburdened now that he had a home for the winter, the little bird leaped up into the branches of the affectionate spruce, and the pine tree, true to his word, kept the wind at bay. When the juniper tree heard about the bird's plight, she extended the hand of friendship by inviting the little bird to eat her berries.

"Juniper berries are very good for little birds!" she reminded her new friend.

The little bird was very content in his warm nest protected from the wind with juniper berries to eat. What more could a bird ask for?

The other trees at the edge of the forest commented to each other: "I would never accept a stranger in my home, especially a strange bird," nattered the birch; "I wouldn't trust a stranger with my acorns," chimed the oak; "I do not trust the stranger," said the willow. They stood proud and tall, but when evening fell, the winds came out to caress the leaves of the trees. As the North Wind blew his soft, cold caresses, the leaves shivered and fell to the ground. The wind wanted to caress every leaf in the forest, especially because he loved the sound of the swishing leaves. He called out to his father, the Frost King, "May I caress every leaf?"

"Oh, no, my son," cried the Frost King. "I would like you to be sure not to caress the trees which extended a hand in friendship to the injured bird. They may keep their leaves."

The North Wind obeyed his father and left them alone. The spruce, the pine and the juniper tree kept their clothing throughout the winter. Ever since that winter, because of their kindness, the spruce, pine and juniper trees were allowed to keep their clothing all winter.

THE LEGEND OF THE THREE PURSES

Imagine loving someone and not being able to be with them. Well, such was the case of three beautiful, young women, daughters of an impoverished noble man. They were so poor that the family could barely afford to buy food and clothes. Despite finding good men for each of the daughters, the young women were unable to marry because their father could not provide a dowry.

This moving story one day came to the ears of Nicholas, Bishop of Myra. The family's circumstances were so bad that the father could no longer afford to buy food. He was deeply saddened and embarrassed by his situation. The daughters wept continually because they were so hungry and so cold.

Bishop Nicholas decided to do something to rescue this sad family from their suffering. He took some gold and tied it securely in a purse. In the dark of the night, he set off for the poor family's home. While the young women were sleeping, Bishop Nicholas visited the house. Their father was so sorrowful that he could not sleep, so he watched over his sleeping daughters. As it happened, the window of the room in which the girls slept was open. Bishop Nicholas tossed the purse through the window. It landed on the bed of the sleeping women.

The father heard the noise and rushed into the room to investigate. He found the purse and opened it quickly. To his amazement, the purse contained gold. The excited man woke his daughters to share the good news. He gave most of the gold to his eldest daughter for her dowry. As she wed her beloved, her smiles showed everyone assembled how great was her happiness.

But wait! Saint Nicholas was not done yet! He had more gifts to offer. A few

nights later, he filled another purse with gold. And just like the first visit, he went to the noble man's house and hurled the purse through the open window.

The father heard the noise and rushed into his daughters' room. He was astonished to find a second purse filled with gold. The man was so happy that he gave most of the money to his second daughter so she could have a dowry to marry the young man whom she loved.

The noble man was grateful to the benevolent person, the person who blessed them with purses of gold tossed into the room. He couldn't help being curious and want to express his gratitude to the kind person.

The father decided to watch for the generous benefactor the next night. He kept vigil under the open window, waiting patiently for the deepest part of the night. And sure enough, good Saint Nicholas came bearing his gift. As he arrived for the third time, bearing a silk purse filled with gold, he prepared to toss the purse into the open window. The noble man caught the saint by his robe.

"Oh, good Saint Nicholas, tell me why you hide yourself from me? I am so very grateful for your generosity. My daughters are now the happiest of women!" Tearfully, the noble man kissed the saint's hands and feet. Saint Nicholas was so overwhelmed by the commotion of being found out that he asked the father of the girls to help him keep his secret – no matter what the circumstance. The man readily agreed. As before, this third gift allowed the youngest daughter to be able to marry her beloved.

And so it was said that the three daughters and their father lived their lives in contentment and happiness ever after.

THE CHRISTMAS THORN OF GLASTONBURY

This legend is from Britain, known as an Oldie Goldie Christmas folktale.
Retold

According to this legend, there was a very righteous man by the name of Joseph of Arimathea. It is said that he offered his own prepared sepulchre to Our Lord Jesus Christ when the crucifixion was over and our Lord's body needed a burial place. This good and caring man was also persecuted by Pontius Pilate, and for that reason Joseph of Arimathea fled Jerusalem, carrying with him the Holy Grail, which he carefully hid beneath a samite cloth. At the time, samite was a luxurious, heavy silk fabric often woven with gold or silver threads.

Joseph of Arimathea roamed the land not knowing where his faith would take him. Whenever he was tired, one could see him leaning his tired body on a rod fashioned from a white thorn bush. He travels took him through all kinds of landscapes: enraged seas, lifeless wastelands, rugged forests, rocky mountains and rapid-running rivers. At last he came to Gaul where the Apostle Philip was preaching the glad tidings to the heathen. Joseph decided to stay there for a short while.

One night, while sleeping in his abode, Joseph was awakened by a bright light. In his startled, half-awake state of mind, he saw within the light an angel hovering by his couch enveloped in a cloud of incense.

The angel said, "Joseph of Arimathea! Arise thou, and cross over into Britain. Preach the glad tidings to King Arvigarus. In that place, a Christmas miracle shall come to pass when the first Christian church is built in that land."

Joseph lay on his couch, confound and wondering what sort of answer he should give the messenger, but the angel had already departed.

Joseph hurriedly left his home and went to find Philip. He shared the angel's message with Philip, who helped him gather eleven trusted followers to accompany Joseph to Britain. Philip bid the men good luck and sent them on their way. The band of men travelled toward the river where they found a little ship that could take them to the coasts of Britain.

When they arrived in Britain, Joseph of Arimathea and his followers were met by an unbeliever who showed them the way to meet King Arvigarus. The king gave Joseph the opportunity to preach the glad tidings to the king and his subjects, but though the king's heart was softened somewhat, he was not convinced by Joseph's message. However, the king was a generous man, so he granted Joseph and his followers the island of Avalon, also known as the happy isle and the isle of the blessed, and sent the group there to build an altar to their God.

This island – the wonderful gift of Avalon – also had another name: the Island of Apples and called by the islanders, the land of Ynis-witren, the Isle of Glassy Waters. It was a truly beautiful and peaceful place to establish God's altar. The site of the altar was in the midst of a green valley where warm breezes filled the air with the scent of apple blossoms and ripened fruit. The green grass was as soft and lush as a carpet, and the gentle waves splashed the shore while water-lilies danced on the tide. Above, soft fluffy clouds dotted a blue sky.

It is said that Joseph of Arimathea and his followers arrived on the Isle of Avalon on the holiest day of the year, Christmas Eve. Of course, they had

brought with them the Holy Grail, concealed in a covering of snow-white samite. Their feet felt like lead as they trudged up the hill called Weary-All, but once they reached the summit, Joseph cast his thorn-staff into the ground.

To everyone's surprise, a miracle unfolded before their eyes! The thorn-staff sent out roots, which sprouted and budded, and burst into bunches of white, fragrant flowers! This was the very spot of which the angel had spoken in Joseph's vision. On this site, Joseph of Arimathea erected the first Christian church in Britain. The walls of the church were built using rows of upright stakes made from willow osiers gathered at the water's edge. It was always believed that in this chapel, the Holy Grail was concealed. The church afterwards became known as Glastonbury Abbey.

Legend has it that ever since that auspicious day at Glastonbury Abbey, the white thorn buds and blooms on Christmas Eve.

THE SLEEP TREE

The Aboriginal people of North America Retold

The Aboriginal people of North America from the north, south, and central regions of the continent, are rich in traditions and myths depicting a partnership between nature and people.   When the "Great Invasion" of the Europeans overtook and destroyed large portions of the aboriginal world, the underlying truths about nature remained.   These truths are recorded in the myths and traditions of a wide variety of people across the Americas, known collectively as Native Americans, or First Nations people.

This legend represents one example of the richness of Native American stories which teach and inspire us to find our personal place in the living natural environment. As science continues to keep us informed about the outcome of our actions on our environment, this motivation and knowledge must always go hand-in-hand with constant guidance. This management begins with the decisions we express about ourselves and our actions. It extends to neighbourhood, community, region, nation, and world. It is a challenge to each of us to become sincerely involved in the stewardship of nature.

"The Sleep Tree" comes to us from the people of the Amazon rain forests of South America. Theirs is a plight suffered by Native Americans across the hemisphere, one that is both tragic and dramatically different from other aboriginal people around the globe. Though rain forests around the globe are being destroyed, nowhere is the impact greater than in the rain forests of the Amazon.

Having lived close to the rain forests of Guyana, South America, I can recall experiencing the amazing mixture of life "under the canopy." I hear the cry of the Native Americans of the Amazon: their genuine fear of the diseases and death that has encroached upon them by the daily destruction of their world; the greed for more farming and homes that takes its toll on the environment; the continued displacement of wildlife through loss of habitat; and the growing extinction of creatures in the name of modernization and development. "The Sleep Tree" is a very old legend from the Karaja and Apinaye natives of the rain forests in the central and northern Amazonian terrain. There are two versions of this legend.

The Sleep Tree – version one

A hunter, whose name was Uaica (U-ai-ca), was out wandering when he came to an unexplored part of the rainforest which spread not far from his village. He noticed an enormous tree that he had never seen before. The large roots were buried deep into the ground. Its limbs spread open like an umbrella over a wide area. The limbs were most welcoming to all animals living among is branches. There were the monkeys, birds, and other living animals that inhabited its rich foliage. It was very tall, as if the branches were reaching up into the sky far above the canopy of the rain forest. The tree gazed down upon all growth below over the centuries of its long life. It was so old it could have very well been the grandfather of all the trees in the surrounding forest, which all the dwellers of the forest had enjoyed over the many years. This tree stirred Uaica's curiosity, and he began to examine this wonder before him.

To his amazement, Uaica saw that there was a large group of animals all sleeping peacefully underneath the branches of the ancient tree. Trees were revered among his people, since they offered great medicinal benefits for the tribe. Uaica had a hunch that he was witnessing the sacred as he gazed in wonder upon the lofty tree. Discovering that tree was a spiritual experience for Uaica. Just to be in the presence of this immense forest tree whose age must span centuries, maybe even thousands of years drew Uaica into a sense of the tree's mystical being. He began to feel sleepy and could not resist the temptation to join the animals on the ground enjoying the shelter of this divine tree.

Before he knew it sleep had overcome him, and Uaica was also sleeping peacefully like the other animals. His sleep was full of dreams unlike any he had ever before experienced. In these dreams, strangers he did not recognise and animals of which he knew nothing appeared to him. An ancestor of his people, Sinaa (Si-naa), spoke to him. He showed Uaica the land of his forefathers and imparted to him many sacred things; knowledge usually shared with teachers, healers and the medicine people of his tribe.

When he finally awoke close to sunset, Uaica got up and hurried home. He kept his experience to himself. Curiosity could not keep him away from the ancient tree. The following day, he returned to the sacred place under the tree, and once again he fell asleep under the marvellous tree. As before, he entered his ancestral world, and was imparted with knowledge by the healer Sinaa. This behaviour continued several times as Uaica would return to the tree. He fell asleep and entered the world of knowledge through the tree. It was a journey of secret knowledge and his lessons became more intense.

Then one day his ancestor Sinaa told Uaica that he must let this visit be the last to the sacred tree. Uaica recalled the message upon waking. He was warned that he would be in danger if he returned to the world of his ancestors. He gazed unhappily at the tree he knew he would never see again. As a parting gift, Uaica took some bark from the ancient tree and protected it among the sacred objects he collected in a bag and which he always carried with him. On his return to his village, Uaica dipped some of the bark into the river close to his home. He felt a deep abiding respect for the river that had given such an abundance of life to the forest and to his tribe.

Uaica decided to sample the mixture of the water and the sacred bark. It tasted bitter. At first, he thought something magical would happen. Much later, he discovered the effects of the drink. It caused him to hop about as if in a daze. His restlessness brought Uaica to the river, where he caught some fishes. As the effects of the drug wore off, Uaica returned to his village.

Afterwards, Uaica was careful to obey his ancestor's dictum not to return to the mystical tree. However, he did continue to explore the secrets of the tree's bark. As it happened, a child of the village fell ill and the medicine man of the tribe was unable to cure the child's sickness. Knowledge of the mysterious bark had spread among the members of the tribe, so the medicine man brought the child to Uaica. He knew he could cure the sick child because the knowledge had been imparted to him by Sinaa while he had slept under the tree. Uaica could heal the child and make the child well again.

After this incident, more of the villagers came to him when they were sick. Uaica healed them back to health in their forest home. He thought his dreaming might end because he was unable to sleep under the mystical tree, but in time, Uaica's dreaming returned and he was able to connect to the wisdom of the ancestors without sleeping under the ancient tree. Stories of his amazing abilities spread throughout the rain forest.

Uaica's life continued in this uncomplicated way until he decided to get married. Unfortunately, for him, Uaica's wife was dissatisfied with her lot in life and began to complain bitterly about everything. Her negative attitude so annoyed her mother-in-law that she ran the younger woman out of the village and told her to go find herself.

The wife's relatives became bitter and vowed to kill Uaica. As he sat down to eat, Uaica's brother-in-law sneaked up behind him, intending to kill him with one blow. Because of his training, Uaica could sense impending danger. He had learned how to disappear right before his assailant's eyes. He took with him his house, his garden, and all of his possessions. After what seemed to be a fruitless search for many days, the villagers found Uaica a long way from the village preparing a new place to live in another part of the forest. The villagers pleaded with him to return to the village. He agreed, and for a while, his life became normal again, but not for long.

Having heard that Uaica had returned to the village, his brother-in-law attempted another assault, intending to kill Uaica. Like before, his training helped him to save himself from imminent danger, and once more, Uaica vanished before the man's eyes. As he disappeared, Uaica warned the perpetrator that his evil actions would now rob the village of their medicine man, whose gifts were given by their ancestor Sinaa as he slept under the mystical tree in the forest. The village would no longer benefit from the lessons Uaica had learned and the tribe would no longer benefit from the healing that came from the sacred bark of the mystical tree.

So it is believed to this day by the villagers that Uaica had vanished into the rock upon on which he was sitting. The tribe believes that he still dwells within the rock. It is also said that from time to time a hand stretches out from the rock, inviting a special dreamer to go into the world of the ancestors to learn the many benefits of the Sleep Tree.

The Sleep Tree – version two

The Aboriginal people of North America Retold

There was once a boy named Uaica, who was very small in stature and of poor health. Pursuant to this disadvantage the other boys in his tribe bullied him every day. His grandfather tried his best to protect his grandson. However, he was not always available to do so and the young boy would walk home through the rainforest.

One day, he decided he would saunter home through the jungle and gaze up into the beautiful canopy of the rainforest which teamed with wildlife. He looked at the leaves, the orchids, monkeys and birds as well as many more animals that called the forest their home. Distracted, Uaica stumbled over something. When he looked down, he was shocked to see a tapir that seemed to be sound asleep. To his even greater astonishment, a sloth lay sleeping next to the tapir. In this fashion, monkeys, a caiman, a jaguar family and a huge anaconda slept together beneath a huge tree. The limbs of this tree were so huge that they spread a green canopy over the sleeping animals and the boy below. The light passed through the leaves, creating speckled patterns and the branches were decorated with brightly-coloured, fragrant flowering vines. The scent caused the birds to feel so happy that they sang sweet melodies all day long. Uaica, too, felt happy and content, but he couldn't help wonder what could be the cause of all this joy and contentment. He stepped closer to the tree. He began to feel very tired and drowsy. He yawned and his legs slowly lowered his fatigued body to the ground. Making himself comfortable, Uaica joined the other animals on the ground and soon was sound asleep. This sleep would turn out to be a life-changing experience for him.

Falling into a deep sleep, Uaica started to dream about animals. Some were familiar to him, but others were not. Then, his dream filled with people, including members of his family, his friends and some strangers, too. Everyone sat together singing in harmony. An old man got up and came toward him.

The old man introduced himself. "I am Sina-a, child of Jaguar."

Uaica knew of this Jaguar Man because he had always been thought of by his people as a great teacher. Sina-a began to tell stories and Uaica listened with rapt attention. He heard how Jaguar Man had cheated eagle of his fire; how Jaguar Man had created a plant for food from the remains of dead snakes; and even how Jaguar Man had once owned all the night so that Earth was in a state of constant daylight.

When Uaica awoke, the sun had set and it was nearly dark. The animals had vanished and he was alone under the tree. Uaica ran home in the fading light. (Some versions of this story claim that he slept into the early hours of the morning.)

The following day, Uaica was eager to return to the tree. He became obsessed with the flat surface under the tree and lay down for another sleep. Very soon, he was sound asleep. He had the same experience as the previous day. Enchanted by the animal sounds and the singing, he eagerly listened to the Jaguar Man's stories. As before, Uaica slept into the early hours of the morning. This behaviour continued for several days with Uaica leaving in the early hours of the morning and returning every evening.

In his dream, the Jaguar Man observed that the boy was becoming very frail and thin. Concerned about Uaica's physical state, he warned the boy not to return to the tree to enter his world. He must stay away. Otherwise, a time might come when Uaica would not be able to leave the Jaguar Man's dream world.

Uaica reluctantly agreed.

Back in the village, Uaica's grandfather wondered about his grandson as he prepared some food for the boy. Upon his return, the boy was hungry. His grandfather fed him and then enquired of him. "Where have you been going?" asked the anxious grandfather. "You depart early, before breakfast, and return late when there is no food left." Uaica confessed to his grandfather how he had been spending his days. He described the tree and the animals to his grandfather and told the things he learned from the Jaguar Man.

The next day, the boy and his grandfather went into the forest to see the great tree. "There, grandfather! You go walk under that tree, and there you will understand my journey." Uaica remembered the words of Jaguar Man, and was very careful to stay a safe distance from the tree.

It was not long before the grandfather fell into a very deep sleep, and soon afterward, the animals gathered around him in the peace and solitude, also sleeping deeply. Uaica was almost persuaded to join them under the tree, but he remembered the Jaguar Man's warning and stayed away.

His grandfather slept for a short while, but when he awakened, he seemed visibly upset. He said to Uaica, "Never impart your knowledge of this tree and its powers to anyone. It is very powerful and anyone who sleeps under this tree must be very strong with their own power of the forest deep in their hearts. Should someone not be strong enough in their own heart and full of integrity, they might seek the knowledge from the dreaming tree for their own selfish desires. They could do evil. You are strong in spirit, Uaica. Now you must eat and be strong in body, also. It is time for you to stay away."

So Uaica heeded the words of Jaguar Man and his grandfather.

Upon their return to the village, they were given word that a boy named Xibute had fallen ill. Uaica knew this Xibute well for he had been one of his tormentors. No cure could be found for the ailing boy, and it appeared that he would die. However, Uaica, having spent time with Jaguar Man, had learned the gift of healing, so he laid his healing hands on Xibute and he became well again.

People in the village could not believe the powers of this small boy, Uaica, who could have any powers he wished. However, after the cure of Xibute, sick people came in search of Uaica. He continued to heal the sick with his healing hands.

Having been pleased with Uaica's obedience, the Jaguar Man appeared to the boy in a dream one night. He told Uaica, "You have passed my tests. You obeyed and stayed away from the dreaming tree, as I requested of you. I was very pleased to see you showed kindness toward your enemy. Now I will impart to you more powers so that you may take care of your people as I once did."

Every night thereafter Uaica united with Jaguar Man in his dreams. He was taught more of the healing secret ways and was given more wisdom, continuing the lessons that he had started at the sleeping tree.

His grandfather provided Uaica with his own special house, a place of solitude to sleep and to dream. Together they planted a garden of special, healing plants. In the meantime, Xibute – the boy who had been his tormentor – became his closest friend and helper. Xibute knew that not only had his body been healed but most importantly his heart had grown full of love like the river of the great Amazon during the rainy season.

As time went on, Uaica's knowledge grew deeper, and he could see beautiful things in his journey of dreams, things he had no knowledge of before – things that he thought would be wonderful gifts for his friend, Xibute and his grandfather such as brightly feathered necklaces, headbands and bracelets. With this knowledge imparted to him, while he was awake he created beautiful things using bright feathers and shells, nuts and bones and animal fur. His dreams inspired him and taught him some brilliant ideas no one in his tribe had ever attempted before.

Unfortunately, there were some very envious members of his tribe who only had negative thoughts for Uaica. When these people saw his handiwork, they were so jealous that they forgot that with some help from Uaica they, too, could turn out beautiful works of art. Instead, their hearts were filled with negative thoughts, "He thinks he is better than us!" and with that they began scheming among themselves to find a way to destroy Uaica.

The haunting question was, how would they carry out this despicable act?

They decided amongst themselves to wait until Uaica was having his meal. They concealed themselves out of everyone's sight close to Uaica's house. Later that afternoon, the hidden people could see Uaica and his grandfather returning from a fishing trip. Uaica held a fish in his hand and it was going to be their supper that night. The hidden ones watched and waited quietly while Uaica prepared the fish for cooking. When he and his grandfather sat down to eat, his enemies crept out of the bushes to launch the assault.

Just as a tribesman was about to hoist his club, Uaica unexpectedly stood up. He spoke to the man. "I have cultivated many skills in the dream world. I am able to see what is happening even behind me." Without any further word, Uaica vanished from their sight, along with his grandfather and Xibute. The house and garden disappeared, too. His enemies were shocked and left speechless.

Uaica possessed the ability to transport himself from one place to another in the blink of an eye.

The elders of the tribe were most concerned since no one had his powers of healing. They went in search of the family.

The tribe found him in a distant place. They pleaded with Uaica to please come back to the tribe. After much imploring he agreed to do so. However, it wasn't long before his enemies surfaced again and began plotting to destroy him once again. They had a master plan. Part of this plan was to host a great feast in honour of Uaica. But it was all a big lie. Just like before, when one man raised his club over Uaica's head, the victim caused a large crack to open in a rock. All of his family and all of his possessions disappeared into the crevice of that rock. As the men of the village looked on in astonishment, only Uaica's voice could be heard. He bellowed from deep within the rock, "Be sure to know that we will never return to you since you cannot appreciate the gift we bring to your tribe."

The three men were never seen again.

SIR GAWAIN AND THE GREEN KNIGHT

This is a legend from the period when Camelot was still young, a very, very long time ago. Retold

Imagine being at a New Year's Party and your host decides he will not eat until something unusual happens!

King Arthur was a very young and a restless man. He and his Queen, Guinevere, hosted a New Year's feast given in honour of the Knights of the Round Table and their female partners. It was certain to be a grand affair. However, their King, being young and restive, decided he was not going to eat until something amazing happened – something that was mind-blowing!! Therefore, if King Arthur, their host, would not eat, then none of his guests at the feast would be impolite and touch their food either. To pass the time and forget about their hunger, the guests amused themselves with jokes and polite conversations.

Before the meal became cold, the tension was broken when the doors to the great hall flung open, and entering in along with the chilled air a proud knight rode into the hall, a mysterious nobleman dressed in green, riding a green horse, and wearing no armour. In one hand, he held a sprig of holly and in his other he carried an unusual, green battle axe. Then, as though he was officiating over this feast, he demanded to know the host of the feast.

King Arthur stood and affirmed, "I am the host!"Then he inquired of the uninvited guest, "If you come in peace, you are welcome in this hall. However, if you come for battle..."

The Green Knight laughed. His laughter echoed through the hall, as he said, "I come in peace. If I came for battle none of your loyal children would be able to rise against me." The King was becoming impatient and it was obvious from the change of his facial expression, as it had turned red with anger. There was a general dragging of chairs as all the knights stood in respect to their host. Then King Arthur demanded of the stranger, "Why do you come? And who are you?"

The stranger replied, "I am the Green Knight, and I come to propose a challenge." He held his battle axe up in the air and continued, "I am giving you the chance to swing this axe and sever my head. However, next year at this same time I will ask the same in return. That is, you must present your head to me and let me return the act of unfriendliness to you."The gaze of the emerald giant penetrated the assembly when he demanded, "Who will accept my offer?"

Apart from the rustling of people stepping back, there was a tense silence in the hall. Once again, the Green Knight laughed. His laughter echoed through the hall. "Children undeniably. And cowards as well!" Just then, King Arthur declared, "I will accept your challenge, and I will swing the axe!" He stepped forward to raise the weapon.

Standing at Queen Guinevere's side was Sir Gawain; as noble and handsome as any knight any king could hope to be. He rushed to his King, fell to his knee, and offered himself, "Your Highness, please allow me the honour because your life is far too costly to sacrifice to this knight."

With his body language King Arthur handed over the axe. Green Knight, not wasting any time or words, requested of Gawain, "Make the blow count," as he stepped aside. The young knight Sir Gawain stood up and faced the giant stranger. "Where are you from, Good Sir?" he respectfully asked the Green Knight. The Green Knight looked at the young man in a positive manner and warned him, "I will let you know once you have struck the blow."Gawain looked confused over the words of the Green Knight. However, once the Green Knight had bowed his head the young knight lifted the axe. He swung the axe very intentionally and deliberately.

Needless to say, Sir Gawain gave a powerful swing. It was a grizzly scene as the decorated head rolled across the hall, frightening many of the knights and their ladies. They were even more speechless and frightened much more when the body of the strange knight stood in search of his head. The Green Knight easily found his head and tucked it under his arm.

To everyone surprise the head addressed Sir Gawain, "Meet me in a year at this same time at the Green Chapel."

The Green Knight, now a headless rider, sharply turned his horse, head and all, and exited the feasting hall as quickly as he entered leaving Sir Gawain holding the emerald battle axe.

To everyone's amazement, the king showed no emotion over the mysterious scene and whatever King Arthur might have felt no one will ever know; rather, King Arthur said to his Queen, "Take courage, My Lady, such cleverness will soon become a Christmas story." As he made his way back to his throne, he paused and told Sir Gawain, "Put away the battle axe. It has displayed enough this day."

Time waits for no man, and so the winter quickly changed to spring. Spring quickly rushed along, bringing new life, and followed closely by warm, lush summer. As the year marched onward, Sir Gawain knew that the time had come to fulfill his promise to meet the Green Knight at the Green Chapel. Not knowing which direction to take, Sir Gawain hesitated, so it was All Souls' Day when he finally bid farewell to his King and Queen and all the Knights of the Round Table and set out on his uncertain journey to find the Green Chapel.

The journey would prove to be very difficult since Sir Gawain met with many obstacles. No one he encountered along the way seemed to know where the Green Chapel might be.

Finally, with the snow falling heavily, and with his horse growing so tired it could scarcely put one hoof in front of the other, Sir Gawain noticed the walls of a castle through the heavy vegetation of the woods. He dismounted and with great effort trudging through the snow, he made it to the gate to ask for generosity from the castle inhabitants. The gatekeeper very willingly opened the gates to welcome the snow-covered young knight and his horse into the courtyard. The domestic staff ran to assist Sir Gawain in removing his armour and to walk the stallion to the stable. Another aide ran to inform the lord of the manor of the arrival of a visitor. It was not long before a gracious host, with thick russet hair and beard, came to greet the knight and escort him to the fall and the fireside.

The host, being the owner of the castle, presented himself as Lord Bertilak, and was most delighted when Sir Gawain introduced himself as a Knight of Arthur's Round Table. As they walked towards the fire in the great fireplace, they met Lady Bertilak accompanied by an elderly aide. The older woman's appearance contrasted greatly with the beauty of the lady of the castle. The polite Sir Gawain greeted each lady with great respect and knightly courtesies.

Lord Bertilak encouraged Sir Gawain to join the feast that was to be held that night and Sir Gawain accepted his invitation. Upon his arrival at the feast, Sir Gawain was given the place of highest honour at the table. At once the feast began and everyone engaged in conversation. Lord Bertilak enquired of Sir Gawain, "Tell me dear Knight, why you ride so far into this forest? A small number of travellers come this way, and even less in the winter."

"I am looking for the Green Chapel, which I must find by the New Year," Sir Gawain responded simply.

"Oh, yes, I see," laughed the Lord. "That is most easy! That Chapel is not very far from here."

"I would be most grateful to you," the young knight begged, "if you could show me the way."

"All in good time," Lord Bertilak answered. "It is still four days before the New Year. Have a rest for a while here and regain your health before adventuring into such a rough trail into the wilds." With that he stood up and announced, "Let us all retire for the night. Before the rising of the sun, I will depart on a hunting expedition."

"Ah, a hunting trip you said kind Lord? May I join you?" asked Sir Gawain.

"No, no! You must rest. Sleep in tomorrow," replied Lord Bertilak. He gestured toward his wife and added, "And when you rise for breakfast, my good Lady will take good care of you." He laughed at his own pun. "However, so you feel a part of it, I offer you a small contest."

"Agreed!" exclaimed Sir Gawain.

"Whatever I capture I will share with you and whatever you profit tomorrow you can share with me," suggested Lord Bertilak.

"Absolutely!" said the young knight.

Many hours after Lord Bertilak had left to hunt deer, Sir Gawain's sleep was interrupted by someone entering his room. He could hear the beautiful Lady Bertilak breathing as she stood by his bed. When she made no effort to leave, Gawain pretended to awake. The beautiful woman propositioned him, but Sir Gawain refused all of her advances as courteously as he could. She persisted in her attentions, and finally, not wanting to offend the lady, Sir Gawain accepted a kiss from her delicate lips.

That evening, Lord Bertilak and his men returned with horses piled high with the meat of the hind. The Lord of the castle presented his share to Sir Gawain. "There you are. Here is my portion of the catch," Lord Bertilak laughed. Then, the knight asked, "And what of you, my lady?"

"Only a kiss, my lord," said Sir Gawain.

The Lord of the castled asked, "How is it that you are privileged with such a pleasant prize?"

The young knight giggled and politely said, "I am sorry, Sir, but that was not in our bargain."

"So very true!" Lord Bertilak said, clapping the knight on his shoulder.

The following day was a repeat of the first day, except that Lord Bertilak brought back the head of a board and Sir Gawain had two kisses to exchange.

On the third day of the third hunt, Sir Gawain awakened to a gray day after having a very disturbed sleep haunted by visions of the Green Knight. To compound his troubles, the unwelcome sight of Lady Bertilak was once again present in his room. As before, the beautiful Lady propositioned him, but Sir Gawain, being a morally respectable man, refused all of her advances as courteously as he could. She became annoyed and asked Gawain, "Are you committed to another Lady?"

Sir Gawain answered, "Absolutely not! How could I be committed to another with the fate that awaits me tomorrow?"

"Well, then," she pleaded, "Give me something of your to remember you."

"My lady, I have nothing to offer," replied Sir Gawain. "All I have is my horse and my armour, and those are needed to take me to the Green Chapel."

Lady Bertilak removed a ring from her finger and gave it to him. "Here is a token to remember me," she said. Sir Gawain replied sadly, "I do not have anything of value to exchange in return."

Lady Bertilak was becoming impatient with Gawain's polite rejections. She removed a green, silk sash from around her waist.

"This is of no value. It is a trivial offering. Please, accept it."

"I cannot," protested the young knight.

"On the contrary, it has supernatural powers that will guard you and protect you from harm," whispered the lady as she bent even closer.

As he fondled the sash, Gawain reflected on the fate that awaited him the next day. His mind filled with the memory of the Green Knight placing his head back on his body and Gawain realized he did not have the same power. "Thank you," he said politely, accepting the gift of the sash. He did not object very strongly when she claimed three kisses from him.

As Lady Bertilak left the room, she begged, "Please promise me you will not mention to my husband about the sash."

"You have my word. I shall not mention the sash," Sir Gawain answered.

When she left the room, Gawain quickly got dressed and went to the castle chapel to pray and to confess.

That evening Lord Bertilak returned from the hunt with a fox pelt. The preoccupied Sir Gawain hastily offered the three kisses, even before the Lord of the castle had said a word about the fox.

Finally, on New Year's Day, Sir Gawain was guided by a servant along an unfriendly, windy trail. As they approached the Green Knight's abode, the servant begged the young knight to reconsider by recounting all of the horrendous stories about the Green Knight's ruthlessness. The servant even offered to lie that Sir Gawain had gone to the Chapel, giving him an opportunity to escape unharmed, but Sir Gawain would have none of it. He angrily sent the servant back down the trail and rode the rest of the way by himself until he came to a deserted mound with only one opening. Not knowing what to make of the sight before him, the knight entered the doorway. Then, he heard a bone-chilling sound: the grinding of an axe. He followed the sound into the heart of the mound. There he found the Green Knight, quite occupied among the torches, grinding a new green axe.

"Ah, you are an honourable man," said the Green Knight. "You've kept your obligation! Now, take off your cloak and helmet, and let us be at our game!"

"Remember, one blow is your only right," Sir Gawain reminded the knight as he placed his head on the block. When the axe was about to come down, the young man flinched.

"What is this?" the Green Knight yelled. "I see you so fear the axe that you would flinch from it!"

Sir Gawain protested, "I did not flinch!"

"I promise I will not flinch or move the next time," Sir Gawain pleaded with the knight. The second blow paused just short of his neck.

"A test! Just testing your nerve to see if you really are ready for this," said the Green Knight.

"Just do it! Strike the blow!" exclaimed Sir Gawain.

"I will indeed," replied the Green Knight as he raised his axe. This time, the axe merely nicked the young Sir Gawain's neck. Upon seeing the trickle of blood upon the floor, he jumped to his feet and brandished his sword.

"That was your one blow!" he cried. "Now, our business is finished!"

"Yes, indeed we are," the Green Knight giggled, leaning calmly upon his axe. "The results could have been much worse for you, but you proved yourself a worthy knight."

"Who are you?" the young knight enquired.

"I am Lord Bertilak, and with the assistance of my Lady Wife, we tempted and tested your worthiness. You see, I held my hand on the first two blows because you refused the propositioning of my wife. I gave you only a nick because you hid the sash from me – though I could not blame you for wishing to save your own life. However, the fact that you kept your promise and did come here, knowing your fate and laid your head upon the block, is what saved your life. You are a worthy man, indeed."

Sir Gawain suddenly felt ashamed and his cheeks flushed red as he pulled the sash from around his waist. He cast it to the ground in anger.

Lord Bertilak said, "No, no, my young knight. Wear it proudly to prove that you faced the Green Knight and lived – and to signify that we parted friends."

"Friends! Yes, indeed. Except I will wear it to remind myself not to be so proud of my abilities and that I, too, am an imperfect man," said the young knight as he picked up the sash. Then, facing the Green Knight, he demanded of him, "Why this test?"

Lord Bertilak gave him this explanation: "The old woman is Morgan le Fay. She is half-sister to King Arthur. She also happens to be your aunt. She induced this fascination upon me so that Queen Guinevere's heart should be distressed and also so that the Knights of the Round Table could prove their bravery." He held out his great, green hand and said, "Which you admirably demonstrated today. So, please come as our friend to our hall and feast in the New Year."

"I thank you," said Sir Gawain humbly. "Now my mission is ended, I must return to Camelot."

When he returned to Camelot, Sir Gawain told King Arthur and the court all about his expedition and his trials. And so it is said that while Sir Gawain wore the green sash to remember humility, the other knights wore green sashes to remember Sir Gawain's courageousness.

THE SILVER PLATE AND THE TRANSPARENT APPLE

A Russian folktale Retold

Once upon a time, many long years ago, there was a peasant and his wife who had three daughters. One daughter was most beautiful, while the other two daughters were not exactly what one would call beautiful. The youngest girl was very simple in every way, even in her taste. She was a good, kind girl, nicknamed Simpleton and everyone who knew her addressed her by that name. In reality, she was very far from being a simpleton.

By comparison, her sisters were very vain. They spent most of their days grooming themselves, adorning themselves with fashionable dresses and jewellery. They didn't have much patience for their youngest sister, and in fact, they didn't get along with her very well. The two oldest sisters made fun of Simpleton by teasing her and mimicking her. The toughest chores were always delegated to Simpleton. She was made to do all the hard work, but Simpleton never complained. Instead, she would willingly complete her chores. She fed and tended the cows and the chickens. She was very kind to others and never refused to do a favour at a moment's notice. In fact, she was a most willing soul.

On day, her father was leaving the house to go to a big fair to sell his hay. He asked each of his daughters what they would like him to bring back as a gift.

"I would like some red fustian (a coarse sturdy cloth made from cotton and flax) to make myself a sarafan (a traditional Russian dress coat)," said the eldest.

The second daughter said, "Buy me some yards of nankeen cloth to make myself a dress."

In the meantime, Simpleton sat in a corner watching her sisters with immense enthusiasm. Although she was a simpleton, her father found it difficult to go on his trip without asking her what her wishes were. To be polite, he asked Simpleton what she would like him to bring her.

"My dear father, would you bring me a silver plate and a transparent apple to roll about on it?"

The father was puzzled by the request, but he didn't say anything about it and departed on his journey.

Then, the two older sisters scolded their younger sister. "What on earth made you request such nonsense?" they demanded, mocking Simpleton.

"Just you wait and see for yourselves when my father brings them!" said Simpleton as she left the room.

The peasant, having sold his hay, purchased the gifts for his daughters and returned home. The two older girls were overjoyed with their presents and giggled at Simpleton, who was waiting to see her present. They could hardly wait to see what she had in mind to do with the silver plate and transparent apple.

The older girls thought she might try to eat the apple, but in this they were disappointed. Instead, Simpleton sat in a corner chanting these words: "Roll away, apple, roll away on this silver plate. Show me many splendour: fields, woods, the seas, the high rolling hills and the heavens in all its glory."

To her sisters' amazement, the apple rolled away and on the plate was the evidence of many foreign towns, one after the other, as well as majestic ships sailing on the seas and lush green fields and meadows. The highest mountains and hills appeared on the plate like a movie. The beauty of the heavens with the rising and setting of the sun was also in plain view on the plate for all to see.

The sisters were astonished. Suddenly, they felt jealous and wanted to have the plate and the apple for themselves. They plotted together, wondering how they could steal the objects from Simpleton since she took such excellent care of them. She cherished this gift so much that she would never want to trade it. Then, one day, an ugly scheme took shape. The wicked sisters persuaded Simpleton to accompany them berry-picking. Simpleton agreed to join her sisters and left her plate and apple in her father's care. They found a lush berry patch at the edge of the forest and soon got to work picking wild strawberries. The three girls had been busy picking berries for some time when the two older girls found a space lying on the grass. After a brief conversation, they put their plan into action. Simpleton continued to pick berries, not paying much attention to her sisters. They crept up behind her and one of the sisters took the spade and dealt their simpleton a severe blow. She suddenly turned frighteningly pale. Then she fell to the ground dead.

Frightened and confused, the sisters picked up Simpleton's body and quickly buried her under a birch tree. Then, they returned home. Because they were late getting home, they concocted a explanation.

"Simpleton has disappeared from us. We looked for her everywhere, but we were unable to find her. She must have been devoured by some wild beasts when we were not paying attention."

The father, who loved his daughter, wept for her. He became very sad. As a way of preserving his daughter's memory, he took the plate and the apple and locked them in a cabinet. The sisters cried bitterly, too, because they realized they were not going to have the transparent apple and silver plate after all. And to make matters worse, they were going to have to share the hard, dirty chores, too.

A shepherd, who was caring for a flock of sheep, lost one of them and went to the edge of the forest to search for it. In the course of his search, the shepherd came upon a small hill under a birch tree. Red and blue flowers grew around the tree and among them, a reed (a perennial grass that has a hollow stem and broad leaves). The caring shepherd plucked the reed and used it to make a pipe. Then, an amazing thing happened. When the shepherd placed the pipe to his mouth, the reed began to play by itself! It chanted, "Play, play, little pipe. Be of comfort to my dear parents, even my sisters, who so heartlessly hit me and killed me. They buried me all for the sake of a silver plate and transparent apple."

The shepherd, distressed about his reed, ran into the village to tell everyone who would listen. A large crowd soon gathered around him wanting to know exactly what happened. The shepherd once again placed the pipe into his mouth. Once again, the pipe began to play by itself. "Play, play, little pipe. Be of comfort to my dear parents, even my sisters, who so heartlessly hit me and killed me. They buried me all for the sake of a silver plate and transparent apple."

"Exactly who was killed, where, and just how?" the crowd wanted to know.

"My good people," called out the shepherd. "I do not know any more than you do. I lost one of my sheep and went into the forest to find it. In my search, I came upon a small hill under a birch tree. Around this tree grew a number of red and blue flowers and among them a reed which I cut off and made into a pipe. The moment I put the thing into my mouth, it began to play by itself and pronounced the words which you have just heard."

As fate would have it, Simpleton's father and sisters were among the crowd that had gathered and heard what the shepherd said. Simpleton's father asked to play the pipe. The shepherd agreed, so he took it and placed it into his mouth. Instantly, the reed began to repeat the words, "Play, play, little pipe. Be of comfort to my dear parents, even my sisters, who so heartlessly hit me and killed me. They buried me all for the sake of a silver plate and transparent apple."

Simpleton's father asked to be taken to the hillock at once. When they arrived there, the father began to dig open the mound. To their amazement, they found the dead body of his youngest daughter. The father fell to his knees and tried in vain to bring his daughter back to life.

The people began asking who had killed and buried Simpleton? The pipe responded, "My sisters asked me to accompany them into the forest and hit me with something all for the sake of a silver plate and a transparent apple. It is possible to wake me from this sleep. You will have to bring me the water of life from the royal fountain."

Immediately, two very frightened, speechless sisters were arrested, bound together and sent to a dark prison. They remained there until the king had determined their fate.

In the meantime, Simpleton's father hurriedly went to the palace. He was taken to see the king's son. He pleaded on bent knee with the prince to have some holy water from the royal fountain. The father explained the entire story and the urgent need for the holy water. The kind prince gave the distraught father permission to take as much of the water of life from the royal fountain as he needed. Then, he told the man, "When your daughter gets better, please bring her to me along with her heartless, greedy sisters."

Simpleton's father was delighted. He expressed his gratitude to the young prince and hurried to the forest with the water of life. Her father sprinkled Simpleton's body with the water several times, and as predicted, the holy water revived Simpleton. Her father was overjoyed to have his daughter awake and standing before him more beautiful than ever. The father hugged his daughter lovingly as the people celebrated and applauded in gratitude.

The following morning, the peasant took his three daughters to the palace to stand before the king's son. The young prince was awed by Simpleton's beauty and asked to see the silver plate and transparent apple. Simpleton showed the prince the silver plate and the apple. Then, she asked him, "Would you like to know the status of your kingdom? Would you like to see that it is in good order; that your ships are sailing; or that there are auspicious comets in the skies?"

"I am willing to hear anything you are willing to tell me, my fair lady."

Simpleton wasted no time rolling the apple round about the plate. There on the plate like a mirror, the prince could see soldiers with various arms, with muskets and flags, drawn ready to do service. As the apple rolled on, waves splashed over the prows of ships as they sailed the seas like a flock of swans with their flags waving in the breeze. The apple rolled some more and the prince saw the splendour of the heavens: the sun, the moon and the stars, and the Milky Way, too.

The king's son was so impressed that he offered to purchase the plate and the apple. However, Simpleton fell on her knees before the prince and addressed him thus: "You may have my silver plate and my apple. I do not desire any money or gifts for them. All I ask of you is that you will forgive my sisters."

The young prince was touched by her pretty face and her honest tears – so much so that he agreed at once to forgive the two heartless sisters. Simpleton was so ecstatic that she embraced her sisters, hugging them around their necks. The Prince took Simpleton by the hand and said, "My fair Lady, I am so impressed with your genuine kindness you have shown your sisters, forgiving them despite their cruel treatment of you. I would like to have you for my wife, provided you agree. You will be known to all my subjects as the Benevolent Queen."

Simpleton replied, "Your Highness, I am touched by the great honour you have afforded me; however, Kind Prince, the final say lies in my parents' hands. If they agree with your request, I would be honoured to be your wife."

Needless to say, Simpleton's parents were delighted to give their daughter their consent and their blessing.

Then, Simpleton said, "I have one more request to ask of you, my Prince. I would like my parents and my sisters to live with us in the royal palace."

The young prince had no objection to Simpleton's request. The sisters fell at her feet, telling her they did not deserve such kindness after all the mean tricks they had played and the unkind words they had said. The following day there was a wedding and much celebration. All of the prince's subjects joined in the festivities, shouting, "Long live our king and queen!"

From that day forward, Simpleton became the Benevolent Queen, who reigned over her subjects with love.

THE MAGIC FIDDLE

A tale from India Retold

There was once a family of seven brothers and only one sister. The brothers loved their only sister very much, but the time came when the brothers had all taken wives. In Indian culture, the daughter-in-law is usually given the chore of cooking for the family since the family unit stays together. The brothers elected their only sister to stay at home to take care of the meals. The wives were very sore over this decision because they were made to work in the fields. The wives were so upset about their situation that they despised their husbands' sister and began plotting how to get her out of the kitchen. The brothers' wives were determined to force her out of the job as cook and provider. The girls were hoping that one of them would be asked to cook instead.

The wives complained bitterly about the fact that their sister-in-law their husband sister was not made to work in the fields. They wondered why the meals were not hot and ready on time since the girl is at home all day. They then called upon their Bonga for assistance; they asked the Bonga to make the girl's water pitcher to vanish when she went to fetch water, and then to make it come back slowly. They even asked the Bonga not to allow the water to flow into the pitcher, and that the Bonga might want to claim the maiden for himself.

What is Bonga? The Santhal religious tribe in India believes that the supreme deity, Thakurji, controls the entire universe. The Bonga is a collection of spirits who rule over the different facets of the world. To be granted their request, people must pacify the Bonga with prayers and offerings. These spirits operate at the village, household, ancestor level of society and even some Bonga are evil spirits that cause disease. A Bonga can inhabit village boundaries, mountains, water, tigers, and the forest.

The sisters-in-laws told the Bonga that at noon when the maiden went to fetch water that the spirit should cause the water to dry up suddenly. "When she starts to cry, allow the water to come back slowly. When the water rises to her ankles, let her try to fill her pitcher, but then reduce the water once more. She will then become so frightened that she will go crying to her brothers.

"Oh! My dear brothers, the water would only reach to my ankles. Still, Oh! My dear brothers, I was unable to fill the container."

Everything happened as the sisters-in-laws had suggested. The water continued to rise until it reached the maiden's knee, but then suddenly went away.

As predicted, the maiden began to cry and complain, "Oh! My dear brothers, the water reaches to my knee! Still, Oh! My brothers, the water jug will not dip."

Then, the water continued to rise. When it reached her waist, the girl cried out again. "Oh! My dear brothers, the water reaches to my waist! Still, Oh! My dear brothers, the pitcher will not dip!"

The water rose and when it reached her neck, the girl cried: "Oh! My dear brothers, the water reaches to my neck! Still, Oh! My dear brothers, the pitcher will not dip."

At length, the water became so deep that the maiden felt herself drowning, and then she cried out once more: "Oh! My dear brothers, the water rose to the height of a man. Oh! My dear brothers, the pitcher begins to fill."

The pitcher fill with water and when it was full, both the girl and the pitcher sank to the bottom and drowned. The Bonga then claimed her and transformed her into a Bonga like himself.

After a while, the girl manifested herself as a bamboo growing on the edge of the well in which she had drowned. When the bamboo had grown to a very tall size, a Jogi, who was in the habit of walking that way, saw the giant bamboo and said to himself, "This bamboo could be made into a splendid fiddle."(*A Jogi is a musician who plays music to charm snakes.*)

The Jogi came back another day with an axe to chop the bamboo; however, just as he was about to start cutting, the bamboo called out, "Please, do not cut me off at the root; rather, cut higher up."

Being obedient, he lifted his axe to cut higher up, but the bamboo called out once again, "Please, do not cut near the top! Cut lower, at the root."

The Jogi raised his axe to cut at the root as requested, but the bamboo said, "Please, do not cut at the root. Cut higher up." This continued for some time. Eventually, the Jogi became certain that a bonga was trying to scare him and he became angry and impatient, so he cut the bamboo at the root, taking it with him to make into a fiddle. The instrument had a very high quality sound that charmed everyone who heard it. The Jogi took it with him wherever he

went, even when he was begging. He would play his fiddle and at the end of the day, he would return home with a stuffed wallet.

Every so often, the Jogi would make a call at the house of the Bonga maiden when he was making his rounds. The Bonga girl's brothers would be strangely affected by the music. Some of the brothers were moved to tears for the fiddle seemed to be crying out to them in pain. The elder brother was so moved that he offered to buy the fiddle. He even agreed to support the Jogi for a year if he could have the charming fiddle. The Jogi cherished his fiddle and refused to sell it.

One day, the Jogi went to the house of the village chief. After entertaining the chief with a few tunes from his fiddle, the Jogi asked for something to eat. Instead, the chief offered to buy the fiddle and offered a high price for it. The Jogi refused to sell it as the fiddle was his means of livelihood. The chief realised that the Jogi would not bargain with him, so he offered the Jogi food and a lavish supply of liquor. He drank so lustily that he soon became intoxicated and fell asleep. While the Jogi was sleeping, the village chief stole the fiddle and replaced it with another old fiddle.

When the Jogi awoke from his stupor, he immediately missed his instrument and suspected that it had been exchanged. He asked for his instrument to be returned to him. The chief and his servants all protested loudly that they had not taken the fiddle. Sadly, the Jogi left the house of the village chief, leaving his fiddle behind. The chief's son, who was a musician, played the Jogi's fiddle and the music it made delighted everyone who heard it.

When all of the occupants of the house were away working in the fields, the Bonga girl came out of the bamboo fiddle and prepared the family meal. After she had eaten her own share, she would put a portion of the food for the chief's son under his bed, carefully covering it to protect it from dust. She would then re-occupy the fiddle.

This routine became an everyday occurrence. The household occupants thought that some young woman was showing her interest in the chief's son, so they were not terribly concerned with finding out who it could be. The young chief's interest was piqued. He determined to keep vigil to find out which of the village girls was being so attentive to his comfort. He thought he should find out who it was and give the girl a good scolding for the grief she was causing. He hid himself in a corner among the pile of firewood.

Soon, the girl came out of the bamboo fiddle and started to comb her hair. After she had groomed herself, she cooked the meal of rice as usual, and having eaten some herself, placed the young man's portion under his bed. She was about to re-enter the fiddle when he ran out from his hiding place and caught her in his arms. The Bonga girl exclaimed, "Fie! Fie! You may be a dom, or you may be a hadi of some other caste with whom I cannot marry!"

Then, the young chief said, "From today, you and I are one." From that moment, the young chief and the girl began to hold conversations with each other. When the others returned home in the evening, they saw that she was both a human being and a bonga, and the couple were very happy.

As time went on, the Bonga girl's family became impoverished and her brothers visited the chief's house. The Bonga girl instantly recognized her brothers; however, they did not know who she was. She brought them a cool drink on their arrival and afterwards cooked a meal before them. Then, she sat down beside them and began to cry sadly. She scolded them for the treatment she had received at the hands of their wives. She related everything that had transpired and she accused her brothers of colluding with her mistreatment.

"You must have known it all along and you did not intervene to help me."

The Bonga girl did not seek revenge on her sisters-in-laws. Instead, she was happy with being able to empower her brothers with the knowledge of her pain.

THE TWIN BROTHERS

A tale from Nigeria Retold

The King of Yoruba, Ajaka, had a favourite queen whom he loved very much. He could hardly wait for the day when his queen would bless him with children, and she did. However, he was most frightened when his beautiful queen gave birth to twins.

The law of the land and the universal custom was to destroy twins immediately after they were born, and their mother, too. The king was distraught and could not find it in his heart to execute his Queen and his children. He secretly instructed one of his noblemen to escort the royal mother and her babies to a distant isolated place where they might live in safety away from any threats.

While living on this faraway land, the twin baby brothers grew to adult men and loved each other very deeply. They were committed to each other in every way so much so they were inseparable and found great pleasure in each other's company. They were so in-tuned to each other that when one would speak the other would finish his sentence, which was merely a small example of how much they were in agreement in every way in their thoughts and preferences.

Their mother would soon pass away but not before she imparted to them the knowledge of their royal birth. The boys became quite sad from this moment and wished their father had not sent them into exile. How they wished that the law of the country had not denied them their right to reign.

Then one day they received the news that the king, their father, had died. Sadly, there were no heirs to the throne. The brothers thought that they should claim their birthright, though they could not decide which of them ought to claim the birthright.

In order to settle the conflict, the boys decided to have a contest. They decided each of them should throw a stone and whoever could cast their stone the longest distance should claim the throne. He would then invite the other to share in the glory of the kingdom.

The youngest brother won the contest and departed for the capital to claim his birthright. Upon arrival, the young twin announced himself as the Olofin's (king's son), and was granted his rights to the throne and was crowned king with the consent of all his subjects. As promised, it was not long after that he summoned his brother to come and join him in the royal palace. His brother came and was given great honour and superiority.

However, the older brother was slowly becoming jealous of his younger brother. His jealousy began to fill his heart, and he began to lose his love for his brother. One day, as they were strolling beside the river, the older brother pushed his brother into the water causing him to drown.

He made up a lie, telling his subjects that his brother was tired of ruling and

had asked him to take his place on the throne, and then he left the country. No one questioned the older brother and everyone accepted the new king. He was crowned king and so ruled the kingdom as he had always quietly, secretly desired.

One day, the new king was strolling by the river, and he walked near the very spot where his brother had drowned. As he watched the river, a fish surfaced from the water and began to sing: "Your brother lies here! Your brother lies here!"

The king's conscience began to bother him and he was genuinely frightened. In this mental state, he threw a heavy stone and killed the fish. The death of the fish was only the beginning of the king's woes. On another occasion, the king was out for his daily stroll and once again he passed the spot where his brother had drowned. The king was waited upon by his nobles and protected by the royal umbrella made from the pelts of rare animals. The river rose in waves and sang, "Your brother lies here! Your brother lies here!"

In great amazement, the courtiers stopped to listen to the river. Their suspicions were stirred and they began a search of the water. To their astonishment, they found the body of the former king in the river.

Ashamed of being discovered and also of the true reason for the former king's disappearance, the king knew he would be rejected by his subjects and ousted from the throne. In disgrace, the king committed suicide.

THE OLD WOMAN IN THE WOODS

A German tale Retold

An aristocratic family was once traveling through the deep forest accompanied by a poor servant-girl. When they were in the midst of the forest, they were attacked by robbers who came out of the thicket and murdered everyone except the servant girl. She was saved because she had the presence of mind to jump out of the carriage and hide behind a tree. When the robbers had all left with their loot, she came out and witnessed the great tragedy. Feeling helpless, she began to cry angrily. In her grief she wondered, "However will a poor girl like me ever cope and what will I do, since I do not know how to find my way out of the forest? This forest is so cruel that no human being can survive in it." She then resigned herself that she would perish at some point in time.

She wandered everywhere not knowing what direction to go, desperately looking for a pathway or road out of the forest, but it was all in vain. As the evening drew near and darkness fell upon her, she decided to take a seat under a tree and prayed that the Lord would protect her through the night. She was quite resolved that she would have to accept whatever came her way.

When she had been under the tree for a while, a white dove flew up to her with a little golden key in its beak. The dove presented the little key to her and said, "Look around and you will see a great tree; in it there is a little lock; unlock it with this tiny key and you will find food enough to keep you from hunger and suffering."

Following the dove's instructions, the girl went to the tree and unlocked it. Inside she found milk in a little bowl and white bread, which she soaked in the milk and ate to relieve her hunger. After consuming the food, she was satisfied. As the roosters began to crow, she knew it was time for her to get some rest, but she had no idea where she should lay her head down.

Just then, the little white dove gave her another golden key and instructed her to go to a certain tree. It said, "Open that tree and in there you will find a bed on which to sleep." She did as she was told and opened the lock on the tree. In there she found a beautiful white bed. She fell on her knees and prayed to God for protection during the night. She lay down and slept knowing that God would take care of her.

After a restful night's sleep, the girl came out of the tree and there to greet her was the same little white dove. Once again, the dove came with another key in its mouth. The little dove gave her the key and showed her yet another tree where she would find clothes. As she opened the third lock, she found beautiful clothing trimmed with gold and other jewels, more marvellous than those of any royal daughter. She did not know what to do or where to go, so she stayed there for some time, and sure enough the dove came every day, providing her with enough to meet all her needs, while she enjoyed a very silent life.

Then one day the dove came to the girl with the strangest request for a favour. The girl felt indebted to the dove and was grateful she could be of some service

to the dove. The little dove said, "I will direct you to a small house. I would like you to enter it. Once you are inside the house you will meet an old woman who will be sitting by the fire and who will greet you with 'good-day. 'Please don't answer her, but let her have her way. You must pass her on her right side. Then you will see there is a door, which will open. Enter the room. You will see a number of rings of every kind lying about. Among them will be rings of every kind with very precious stones. Do not touch any of them. You must look for a plain one, which will also be lying among the others. Please, bring it to me as quickly as you can."

The girl did as she was told: she entered the little house and came to the door. There she saw the old woman sitting just as she was warned who said, "Good-day, my child." The girl was careful not to give her an answer and opened the door. "Where are you going?" demanded the old woman as she grabbed the girl's gown. The old woman would not let go, saying, "That is my house; no one can enter in there if I choose not to let them." But the girl did as she was warned and did not speak to the old woman. Eventually, she managed to get away from her and headed straight into the room.

In that room was a table with a large quantity of rings, which shone and dazzled her eyes. She carefully examined all the rings as she looked for the plain one; however, she was unable to find it. While she was searching for the ring, she saw the old woman. She was trying to sneak out of the room with a bird cage in her hand. The girl perused the old woman and seized the cage out of her hand. When she examined the cage, she noticed a bird sitting inside which had the plain ring in its bill.

Then, with the ring the girl ran quite victoriously home with it. She waited for the little white dove to come and get the ring, but it did not. She patiently leant against a tree, as she waited for the little white dove. As she leaned on the tree, she felt it becoming soft and pliable. It seemed to be letting its branches down. In time, the branches encircled her, she saw two arms, and as she looked on, the tree became a handsome man, who embraced and kissed her passionately, thanking her for delivering him from the spell of the old woman, who was a wicked witch.

The witch had changed him into a tree, and every day for two hours, he would become a white dove. As long as she was in possession of the ring, he was unable to regain his human form. Included in the spell were all of his servants and his horses, who had also been changed into trees. They were all released from the spell and took their places beside him. In gratitude, he took them with him back to his kingdom, for he was a prince, the son of a king. There the couple got married and lived happily in their kingdom.

THE KING AND THE JU JU TREE

This folklore is from Africa Retold.

UDO UBOK UDOM was a famous king who resided in Itam. This happened to be an inland town with no rivers. The king and his wife used the spring behind their house to do their laundry.

King Udo had only one daughter, whom he loved dearly. He was always cautious with her care and treated her very tenderly. She was beautiful and, indeed, grew up to be a delightful young woman.

The king was away from his home for an extended time and had not visited the spring for two years. At the end of this long absence, he visited his old laundry place. To his amazement, he discovered than an Idem Ju tree had grown up all around the spring, making it very difficult to use the water as he used to do. The king summoned fifty of his young men to cut down the tree with their machetes, long sharp knives used in farming throughout the country. It is a good tool for cutting brush and trees because a machete has a strong wooden handle and a long, sharp blade. Cutting down the tree turned out to be a thankless job since it quickly healed its wounds. After working all day, the young men thought the tree was just as overgrown as it had been when the work started! The young men returned to the palace and informed the king that they had been unable to destroy the tree. It was a fruitless job and they didn't seem themselves making any headway with it.

The King was most impatient when he received this news. The following day, the king paid the spring a visit with his machete to try and do the job himself. The Ju Ju tree must have had supernatural powers because as soon as the king began to chop at the tree's branches, a splinter of wood flew into the king's eye. The splinter was very painful and the king cried out in great pain. In anger, the king threw away his machete and returned home, looking for some help. The splinter was so painful that he was unable to sleep for three days.

The king summoned his medicine men and ordered them to cast lots to find out why he was in such great pain. They cast their lots and interpreted them. They decided that the reason for the pain was that the Ju Ju tree was annoyed with the king because he had tried to destroy the tree in order to be able to do his laundry at the spring.

The medicine men then told the king that he must present the tree with a peace offering. When the king asked what the peace offering ought to be, the medicine men said the offering must consist of seven baskets of flies, a white goat, a white chicken, and a piece of white cloth. All of these things must be offered to the tree in appeasement.

The king was desperate for some relief, so he did as he was told. The medicine men applied their lotions to the king's eye, but the eye got worse.

Frustrated with all this pain, the king summoned another group of medicine men. When they arrived at his abode, they told the king they would be unable to do anything for his pain, but they knew one man who lived in the supernatural world who could cure him. The king ordered that this man be summoned at once. The man arrived the following day.

Upon arrival, the latest medicine man wanted to know from the King what sort of incentive was in it for him.

"Before I treat your eye, what are you willing to offer me for my services?" he asked.

King Udo replied, "I am willing to offer you half of my town along with its inhabitants, seven cows and some money."

The spirit man refused to accept the king's offer. The king was in such excruciating pain that in a desperate moment, he asked the spirit man to name his price.

"Name your price! I will oblige you," he said.

The spirit man knew exactly what he wanted and did not hesitate to name his price. "The only thing I am willing to accept as payment is your daughter's hand in marriage," said the spirit man.

The king was greatly stressed when he heard this demand, and so he ordered the man to leave since he would rather suffer from the splinter in his eye than hand over his daughter.

That night, the pain became unbearable, worse than ever. The King's subjects pleaded with him to summon the spirit man once again and agree to his price. They suggested that once the king was well again, he could have another daughter, no doubt. They reminded him that if he died, everyone would lose, including his daughter.

Reluctantly, the king, with a broken heart, once again summoned the spirit man. The king handed his daughter to the spirit man. The spirit man began his work. He hastily went into the forest to gather some leaves, which he soaked in water and ground them up. He poured the juice of the leaves into the king's eye.

"When you bathe your face in the morning, you will be able to find what is disturbing you in the eye," said the spirit man.

The king implored the spirit man to stay the night, but he refused. He took the king's daughter and returned to the spirit land that same night.

Just before daybreak, the king arose and washed his face. To his surprise, he found the small splinter from the Ju Ju tree, which had been the source of so much grief and pain. The splinter fell out of his eye and the pain disappeared. The king felt quite well again.

Once the king was relieved of his pain, the world started getting back to normal. It occurred to him that he had made a terrible mistake. He had given up his most precious gift for the sake of an eye. Feeling terrible grief and guilt over his selfishness, he ordered that there should be a three-year period of mourning for the loss of his daughter.

Little did he know that his daughter was also experiencing great suffering. For two years, the king's daughter was held captive in the house by the spirit man. She was given meals, but a skull that was kept in the house spoke to the princess, warning her not to eat anything. The skull hinted that the girl was being nurtured, but not for marriage; she was to become a feast for the spirit man. When she heard this, the princess refused to eat any meals. Instead, she fed her meals to the skull and lived on chalk.

Then, in the third year of the mourning period, something happened to change the princess' fate. The spirit man brought some of his friends to see the king's daughter. She was told she would be sacrificed the next day and they would celebrate by feasting on her body.

The next morning, the spirit man brought the princess her breakfast. The skull feared for the princess and wanted nothing more than to spare the princess's life, especially since he had overheard the spirit man's conversation. While the princess fed the skull her breakfast, the skull described what was about to happen later in the day. He explained the conversation he had overhead and how the spirit man and his friends intended to feast on the princess. The skull told the princess that the spirit man would be going into the woods with his friends to make preparations for the feast. "This will be your opportunity to escape to your father," said the skull.

The skull gave the princess some medicine that would give her strength for the journey as well as directions for the way home. She would come to a fork in the road. She should drop some of the medicine on the ground and it would cause the two roads to become one. She should leave the spirit man's house by the back door and travel through the wood until she came to the end of the town. She would, then, see the fork in the road. Should she encounter anyone on her journey, she should not speak to them. She should not salute anyone either since that would be a sure sign that she was a stranger in the spirit land. Further, the skull instructed her not to turn around if anyone called out to her. She was to stay focussed on her path until she reached her father's house.

Equipped with the medicine and the skull's advice, the princess thanked the skull for all of his help and she departed. The princess was determined to stay focussed on her journey, and when she reached the end of town, she found the

road as the skull had said. The princess ran for three hours until finally she arrived at the fork in the road. There, she dropped the medicine, as she had been told and the two roads immediately became one, just as she had hoped. The princess pressed onward, staying focused and remembering not to salute anyone, and not to look back, although several people did call to her.

Just about this time, the spirit man had returned from the wood and went to the house. To his amazement, the princess was gone. He enquired of the skull where the princess might be, who replied that she went out by way of the back door. He insisted that he did not have any idea where she had gone. Being a spiritman, he very soon suspected that she had gone home; so he quickly followed his instincts and went in search of the princess, calling out for her all the while.

The Princess heard someone calling out for her, so she picked up some more speed and at last arrived at her father's house. The princess related to her father exactly what the skull had instructed her to order her father to do. He very quickly took a cow, a pig, a sheep, a goat, a dog, a chicken, and seven eggs and divided them into seven parts as a sacrifice, and left them on the road. The skull said, "when the spirit man sees these things, he will stop and not enter the town." The king was happy to oblige his daughter and performed the sacrifice as his daughter had instructed him.

Upon seeing the sacrifice, the spirit man sat down at once and started to partake of it. When he was quite satisfied, he packaged the remainder and returned to the spirit land, leaving the princess in the safety of her father.

When the king was sure that the imminent danger was no longer lurking, and his daughter was safe, he sounded his drums and ordered that from that day onwards anyone who died and entered the spirit land could not return to earth to cure sick people.

THE GREEN HUNTSMAN

A story from Denmark Retold.

In the forest of Gronveld, on the west coast of the Isle of Man, stories were passed on about how it was unsafe to walk at night. The greatest danger was that you just might run into the Green Huntsman! According to the folklore, he rode with his head tucked under his left arm, cruel hounds running ahead of his monstrous horse while he held a spear in his right hand.

Whenever it was reaping time, the farmers spread out a sheaf of oats as an offering for his horse. They hoped that their offering would please the horse and their fields of grain would not be trodden upon. One would think that with these preparations in addition to staying indoors, there would be enough protection.

Then one chilly, wintry night as Harold, the farmer, sat at his evening meal a knock at his door stirred his curiosity, so he answered the door.

Harold's blood turned as chilled as the winter's night when he beheld the spectacle before him. It was the Green Huntsman! The apparition's head was held high with great pride. Harold stared up at the apparition, all manner of green hues emitted from his body, hair and clothing.

The Huntsman stared down at Harold as he ordered him to "Hold my Hounds!" giving him the leashes of several huge, black hounds. Together the Hounds and Harold watched the Huntsman move back and forth on the saddle and ride away.

For two hours or more, chilled Harold stood shaking with fear in his doorway. He stared at the supernatural canines. However, when they turned their gaze on him, Harold shuddered when he saw their blood-red eyes.

Finally, the ground vibrated with the thumping of the horse's hooves, as the mighty Hunter returned to the farmyard. The apparition tucked his spear out of the way. He then hoisted a bundle of greenish seaweed supposedly the hair of the mermaid that was slung across his saddle.

Then the giant ghost hollered in the great accomplishment, "For seven years I have hunted her, and tonight I speared her clear!" He shifted in his saddle and directed his head towards Harold. "Bring me a drink!" he commanded.

Harold, who was shaking in his boots with fear, was trembling so much he could hardly have managed to move close enough to return the leashes to the stately ghost; he fled speedily into the house and poured a large mug of mead. To Harold's surprise, he drank the mead in one gulp.

In gratitude, the Huntsman deposited a gold coin into Harold's hand. However, even the coin had supernatural powers. No sooner had the metal made contact with his flesh, than it burned a hole instantly through Harold's hand.

As the farmer yelled with pain, the green giant howled with laughter. "Now you will have an exceptional story to brag about how you shook hands with the Green Huntsman." The Huntsman placed an empty leash into Harold's other hand as he bragged, "let it not be said I did not pay for my drink."

Harold, still in disbelief about what has just played out before his eyes, took the weathered leash and locked it away after the Green Huntsman left. For many years Harold kept that piece of leather, and his prosperity grew beyond his dreams. However, he did not think very highly of the leash, since he regarded the leash as an unclean gift and finally threw it away.

So according to the folklore, from that hour Harold's prosperity declined and he grew poorer than he ever thought was possible.

MAON AND THE WILLOW

Folklore from Ireland Retold.

Maon, by all rights, should have been the heir to the throne of Ireland. However, greed filled his great-uncle's heart and cost him his birthright.In a mad rage of jealousy his great-uncle Covac killed Maon's father who would have been the successor to the throne since his grandfather was the king on the throne at the time. The deaths of his father and grandfather tormented Maon and consequently, Maon lost the ability to speak.

Maon grew up in exile in Gaul, now France. Despite having lost his connection to the Irish throne, Maon grew up a noble youth. He was in love with Moriath, the princess of Ulster. Moriath wrote a love song for Maon, hoping it would charm him into returning to his homeland. Her father's harpist, Craftiny, helped to arrange the music for the song. When the song was ready, Moriath gave Craftiny some expensive gifts and sent him to Gaul to play her love song to Maon.

In a strange turn of events, Maon found the music so enchanting, so touching, and so charming that his speech returned to him. He was able to describe to the King of Gaul the whole truth about his legacy. Once the King of Gaul understood Maon's plight, he gave the young man an army so that Maon might return to Ireland and re-claim the throne. During an astonishing battle, Maon confronted the assassin and usurper, and slew him.

The druid of Covac, (a druid is a member of the priestly class), soon began to wonder about the identity of this young commander who had brought an army over the seas. The druid began to investigate him. The Gaulish warriors simply called him Maon, which means "mariner". Recalling the dumbness of the young prince, the druid inquired whether the commander could speak.

"Yes, he does speak," came the reply. (Labraidh).

From that moment onward, Maon, son of Ailill, was known as Maon Labraidh, the Mariner who speaks. In time, he married his beloved, Moriath, and they lived happily ever after – for the ten years of his reign.

Maon liked to talk about himself, but he never talked about his ears. He was not very proud of his ears because he thought them unimpressively long. No one ever saw Maon's ears because they were always hidden discreetly under his hair. Once a year, Maon had a barber come to trim his hair. The barber was always put to death afterwards so that he could not reveal anything about Maon's ears.

One year, the son of an unfortunate, poor widow was chosen for the job. The grieving mother managed to convince the king to have mercy on her son and let him live. King Maon agreed, on one condition: that the man would swear by the wind and the sun never to reveal to anyone what he might see. The young man gladly met the terms and conditions of the job and when Maon's hair was trimmed, he was returned to his mother.

Not long after, the burden of keeping the secret began to cause the young

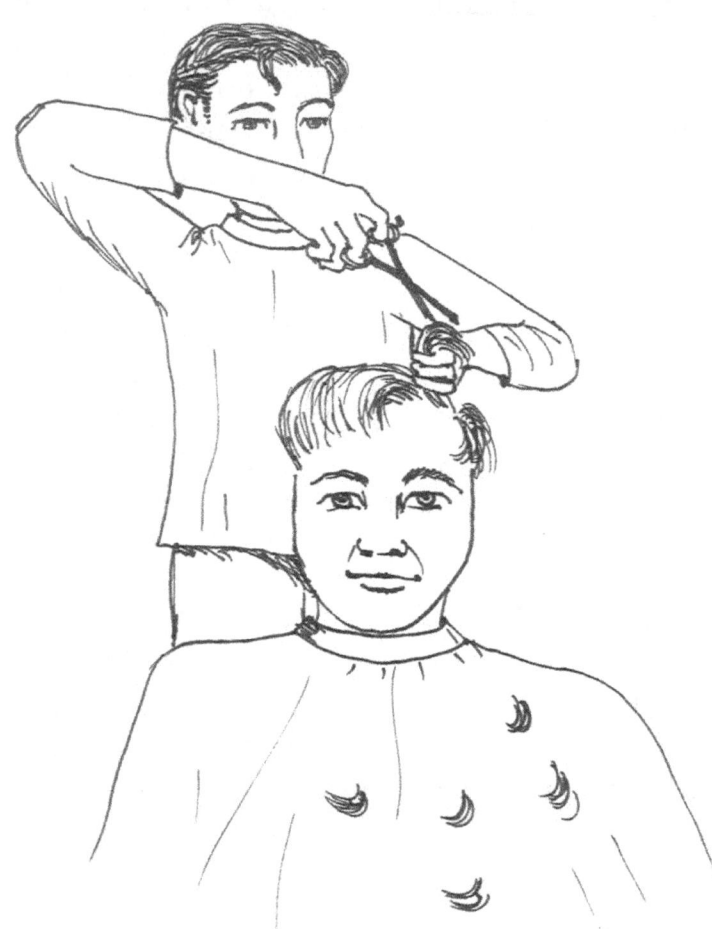

barber to feel ill. He became very, very sick. A wise druid was summoned and advised the young barber to travel to an inaccessible place in the woodlands and to speak softly the secret to a tree. The sick young man agreed to do as he was advised and when he got into the woods, he chose a beautiful, mature willow tree. The young barber quickly told the willow his secret and soon he began to recover from his sickness.

At the same time, the harpist, Craftiny, the very same man who was so influential in reuniting Maon with his country and with his beloved Moriath, decided he needed a new harp. He went into the woods to select a tree from which he would make his new harp. He looked at all the trees throughout the woodland and finally decided upon a willow tree. It just so happened that the willow tree Craftiny chose to become his new harp also happened to be the same willow tree to which the young barber had revealed his secret.

When Craftiny's harp was finished, he was expected to play his new instrument in the king's hall. As the harpist touched the strings, something embarrassing happened. Instead of beautiful music, the new harp spoke: "Two horse's ears have Labraidh the Mariner!" The king became colourless with humiliation and angrily exposed his ears.

The revelation wasn't as bad as Maon had always feared. As he looked around the hall, he recognized that many of his subjects shared characteristics with animals. No barber ever lost his life ever again, either. It goes to show that things are never as bad as we think they might be, and that most of what we fear has to do with our own thoughts. What must have been going on in Maon's thoughts, the King of Ireland, the Mariner who speaks?

All of the barbers of Ireland rejoiced since they could live happily ever after.

CROOKER

An English folktale Retold.

When someone receives a message that their mother is gravely ill, the first instinct is to waste no time getting to her side. This was the situation of one such traveller who travelled to his mother by night instead of waiting until daylight.

The traveller was on his way to Cromford, and along the roadside he met an elderly lady, all dressed in green linen. When she saw the traveller, she called out, "Good lad, where do you travel so late this night?"

Being a very polite man, he explained, "I am travelling to Cromford."

The lady in green advised the man, "I would wait until morning. The road to Cromford is not very safe at night."

The man objected, "I must hasten since my mother needs me this night."

The lady in green then extended a posy to the traveller along with some advice about the journey. "Take these flowers holding out a posy. Once you freed a bird from a Fowler's net and I knew that bird. You will need these to defend Crooker."

"Who is Crooker?" asked the traveller as he took the posy from the green lady. Before she could reply, the wind answered him and the woman had disappeared. The traveller then examined the bouquet of flowers and saw that they were St John's Wort, which is said to be a protection against many ills and evils. Not sure what to make of what had just happened, the traveller continued on his journey. Not long afterward, he met a second elderly lady in green linen.

She called out to him, "Where are you going so late at night?"

He responded, "I am going to Cromford to see my sick mother."

"You once freed a rabbit from a snare, and since I knew that rabbit, I want you to take this posy. You will need it to defend yourself against Crooker." The green lady handed him a bouquet of flowers.

The traveller asked, "Who is Crooker?" as he accepted the bouquet of primroses from the lady. But before he could hear her answer, the wind answered him as the woman had vanished from sight.

The traveller was most grateful for the concern and kindness of the lady. He took comfort in the fact that he now had two posies, not just one.

As the traveller continued on his journey, he encountered a third old woman in green, who also wanted to know where he was going so late at night. Once again, he politely explained the reason for his journey.

She nodded and held out a posy of daisies. She reminded the traveller that he had once rescued a vixen and her cubs from and a trap. She knew them well and as a reward, she was offering him this bouquet of daisies. Like the others, the old woman warned the traveller that he would need the flowers to defend himself against Crooker since he would reach the Cromford Bridge and the shrine before daylight.

Once again, the traveller asked, "Who is Crooker?" Before he could get a reply from her, the wind answered him and the woman had disappeared.

In spite of all of these interruptions, the traveller moved right along. He soon realized that the moon would be high before he arrived at the shrine and the bridge. In spite of the warnings from the old women, the traveller walked unhurried along the treacherous track beside the Darrant River. The traveller feared a slip and fall more than her feared the mysterious Crooker. He could hear the water moaning and bubbling, which sounded like the water was saying "Hungry."

There was an old ash tree at the edge of the path. The moon cast eerie shadows through its branches that looked like grasping fingers. As the traveller walked along, the shadows of the branches seemed to reach for him.

Then he heard the river demand, "Give," and there was a splash.

Remembering his posies, the traveller shouted, "Crooker!" and threw the daisies over his left shoulder as he scampered down the path.

Scared out of his wits, the traveller ran breathlessly forward. However, the branches seemed to reach out toward him almost grabbing his cloak. Then he heard the river demand, "Give," and there was a splash.

Once again, shaking with fear, he grabbed the primrose posy and tossed it over his left shoulder as he took off like a bolt of lightning.

Gasping for air, with his heart pounding as if it were about to jump out of his chest, his lungs on fire and his legs like lead, the traveler journeyed on. He could still feel the intertwining of long shadows as they grabbed at his cloak.

Then he heard the river demanded, "Give," and there was a splash.

Then as if in an act of desperation, he tossed the St. John's Wort straight at the ancient Ash tree, and he threw himself at the shrine. He could still hear the wind rustling, though it could have been the tree.

All night long the concerned villagers could hear the Darrant angrily roaring, and in the morning they came out from their homes whispering, "We must go fetch the Priest" since they were very sure that someone had died through the night.

However, when they came to the Bridge, they found an exhausted and very fatigued traveller praying at the shrine, while the Darrant flowed quietly and smoothly along its banks.

THE LADY IN WHITE

A Czech Tale Retold.

A young Bethushka guided her flock of sheep to graze near a wooded area of birches every day from spring until fall. To pass the time, she took with her in her pocket a spindle for spinning flax into a thread. However, her first choice was to roam and explore in the woods. Often she would take a stroll and gaze upon the new wildflowers that were blooming in the meadow. She was so happy with being in nature that she would make up a little dance, as if she was celebrating the forest, the trees and the flowers just for the fun of it, while she hugged and danced under the trees.

Then one spring day someone interrupted her silence and contemplation. It was a beautiful woman who suddenly became visible in front of her. She was dressed in a silky white dress with long blonde hair, and she wore a crown of flowers on her head.

To the girl's surprise, the woman said, "I see you like to dance!"

"Oh yes," replied Bethushka. "I could dance the whole day! However, my mother has given me this flax to spin while I wait with the sheep."

Then the lady extended an invitation to the girl. "Tomorrow is another day; come, and dance with me! I will teach you some new steps!"

Excited, Bethushka jumped up to her feet and joined the lady. The two ladies were very happy in the enchanted forest as they laughed and sang. They boogied in between the trees and out into the open fields. So springy and happy were their feet the grass was neither trampled nor bent. Then, as the evening was approaching the lady disappeared as suddenly as she had appeared.

The bewildered Bethushka gathered her flock and headed home. When her mother inquired how her spinning was coming along, she pretended to have misplaced the spool. However, not a word was mentioned about the lady in white.

The following day Bethushka returned to the same place, only this time she was determined to do her spinning as her mother had requested. Once again, the lady appeared and asked Bethushka, "Will you dance?"

"I am afraid I cannot dance right now. I have some spinning which I must do; otherwise, my mother will be displeased with me."

"Oh! But if you will dance with me, I'll help you to spin in return."

Hard to refuse such an offer, once again, Bethushka and the lady danced  through the day. Near sunset, the beautiful lady smiled and said to Bethuhska that she should wave her arms. The girl did and just like that the spool was filled with fine linen thread. Bethushka gave her mother the thread that evening and she was very pleased indeed with her daughter. However, Bethushka did not mention anything about her new dancing buddy.

The third day the Lady in White was anxiously awaiting Bethushka's arrival in the woods. Once again, they danced without a care in the world. They practiced their pirouetting and curtseying, whirling and laughing, skipping and swooping. They skimmed over the forest floor as gently as the wind. After a wonderful day, the Lady in White spun the flax again as quickly as a blink of an eye. "You are such a graceful dancer, Bethushka!" She said as she complimented her, "I had so much fun today!" She then presented to Bethushka a pouch with a mysterious pattern embroidered on the front of the pouch. She cautioned Bethushka to take good care of this pouch. Bethushka sneaked a peek inside and saw that it was filled with dried yellow birch leaves.

Upon returning home that evening Bethushka gave her mother the new spool of thread. Only this time her mother looked at the spool very closely.

"This is a well spun spool. Wherever did you get this from? One thing I am sure about is that you did not spin it yourself."

At this point, Bethushka had no choice but to reveal to her mother the whole story about how she met with the beautiful lady dressed in the long white dress.

Her mother exclaimed, "Why, Bethushka, you had the rare privilege of meeting the Wild Lady of the Birch Grove! It's very good luck to the one who encounters her!"

Bethushka then told her mother all about the dancing. "She taught me some wonderful dances!" Then she showed her mother the pouch, "she gave me this dainty little pouch filled up with old birch leaves!"

Bethushka decided to empty the pouch for her mother. Both of them were amazed to see that the birch leaves were made of SOLID GOLD.

THE ANGRY FOREST

A Transylvanian folktale.

After a hard day's work, a group of loggers enjoyed a fire and a chat with each other. Within the ancient Transylvanian forest a crew of woodsmen had laboured all summer, clearing most of one slope, rolling the logs down into the swift, perilous river.

The most senior of the woodsmen, Peter, was fortunate to receive the last bit of the wine they had been sharing. He chanted, "Look! We have given you the first of our wine, and now the last! Please, spare us!"

Upon hearing the conversation Matthew retorted, "Who are you talking to?" Even though he was old enough to know better, he was, however, stubborn enough not to say. Matthew's two sons, Benjamin and Constantine were as modern and obstinate as their father.

Then Peter tolerantly replied, "You know! The spirits have been generous to us this summer, but fall is quickly approaching!"

"We think you are just trying to frighten us more so we'll believe your folktales," Matthew responded. "You know I have no use for your stories. I think we should chop down the last set of trees to get another day's pay."

Benjamin and Constantine nodded in agreement, except the other loggers felt a little awkward and shifted in their seats; some of the loggers were old enough and were inclined to believe as Peter did, while the youngest were unsure of the wisdom behind the folktales.

Peter maintained that these were "Tales that were true," but nonetheless, he knew that no folklore was believable enough to make a man like Matthew believe any of it. Sad to say, whatever Matthew believed so did his boys as they took their cue from their father.

The conversation left everyone feeling very uneasy as they retired to bed that night.

Breaking the silence of the night just before dawn the loggers were awakened to the recognizable sounds of an axe chopping against solid timber. The very concerned woodsmen got dressed and went out to investigate what Matthew and his boys were doing.

Standing beside the last tree trunk, Matthew was having a rest as he leaned against his axe handle. As he greeted the woodsmen, grinning and teasing his co-workers, "It is about time you lazy bones were up! We almost have a whole day's work finished while you slept!"

Still the woodcutters had great reservations as they looked on with fear and uncertainty. They all gazed at Matthew as they shook their heads in displeasure while Matthew lifted his axe to sink it deeper into the trees.

Breaking the silence of the dawn, a strange scream caught everyone's attention. Matthew dropped his axe and hurried toward the grounds were his sons had been working. The rest of the woodsmen quickly followed behind. They arrived in time to see Matthew cradling his youngest boy, Constantine, in his arms. The boy's leg had been cut off by a bear trap that lay beneath a great black oak. No one was able to stop the bleeding, and soon, Constantine bled to death as everyone looked on helplessly.

Not a word was said about Peter's warning, although it was in the minds of each of the loggers. They were all thinking about how the forest spirits demand a sacrifice and get it.

The loggers mourned the death of Constantine and kept an overnight wake in their cabin for him. The following day, they gave him a very simple, uncomplicated burial. Peter read from the Bible and when he was finished, he pleaded with the forest, "Please, be satisfied with one life. Please, let the rest of us go in peace."

"Peter's words angered Matthew. He yelled in great fury to his son, Benjamin, "Grab your axe!"

Benjamin, who was as grief-stricken as his father, wanted to honour his father, so he grabbed his axe and joined him. Both men began chopping frantically at the trees.

The frightened crew of woodsmen tried to console them and to stop them. However, the loggers found their own muscles were frozen. They could only stare helplessly as an apparition rose behind Benjamin, took hold of his axe and plunged it into his skull. Seeing the death of his eldest son, Matthew hollered like a rabid beast. He took hold of Benjamin's bloody axe and frantically hacked at the apparition that was only just visible to him. He kept swinging the axe and chasing the apparition down to the river.

Matthew fell with a loud splash into the foaming river. He struggled between the floating logs, trying not to be crushed by the tumbling logs. The crew, finally released from the spell, all rushed to the water's edge.

They all made the sign of the cross, but no one felt able to fight the logs and the current to save Matthew. They watched in horror as Matthew unsuccessfully fought against the spinning logs.

The loggers feared the worst because they knew there was not much hope. A raft appeared among the logs, piloted by an old man. Matthew grabbed hold of the edge of the raft. The loggers watched breathlessly as Mathew tried to climb aboard the raft. Oddly, the old man took no notice of his passenger. The crew whispered prayers as they observed the infuriated woodcutter fighting to pull himself aboard the raft. The situation became even worse when the onlookers saw a large tree trunk zooming through the old man.

Then the evitable happened: the trunk crash into Matthew, hitting him hard in his chest as he strived to get to his feet. The force plunged him beneath the water.

The following day, after burying Benjamin, the loggers found Matthew's body washed up on the shore. They were grieving loggers who laid him to rest beside his sons.

Then the crew offered prayers to the spirits of the forest, hoping they had drunk enough blood. Then they departed on a long, weary journey through the forest to their homes.

WHEN THE BEMBÖLE PEOPLE WENT TO HARVEST LOGS

A folktale from Finland Retold.

Once upon a time, the settlers of Bemböle decided to construct a new log house in Bemböle. However, to build such a house, they would need logs with which to construct it. Just then another realization hit the people: they would have to go into the forest to harvest the lumber that is needed for the log house.

They set out with a horse-drawn sledge and their axes. One of the settlers told the others that the smartest man should be the privileged to have the sledge and the horse. The other settlers thought that since he thought of the ideas, he must be the smartest, and so he was given the privilege of the sledge. Without hesitation, he took off with the horse and his axe in the sledge.

Content with the decision, the other settlers started off walking, following the sledge. However, it wasn't long before the other settlers lost sight of the sledge. On his ride on the sledge, the smart villager hit a bump in the dirt road and lost control of the sledge. The axe flew off and was left lying on the road. However, since no one has eyes behind their head, the smart man had no idea that he had lost his axe in the jolt.

The other villagers soon reached the spot where the axe lay on the road. They all assumed that the smart one deliberately left his axe behind and they all left their axes also, saying, "Since he is smart and he thinks he does not need his axe, then we do not need our axes also," and they continued on their journey into the forest.

After they all had arrived in the forest, they searched and found the spot where tallest and straightest trees were growing. It was now time to start harvesting the lumber by cutting down the trees of choice. However, they all soon realized that they had a problem. They had no axe. "How will we cut the trees down without our axes?"

They all looked at each other not knowing what they should do next. As they pondered the dilemma, the smartest man said, "Since we have no axe to cut the trees, we have to figure out how to break them down!"

"Excellent idea, only how will we accomplish it?" asked one of the settlers.

"Since I am the smartest I guess I will have to figure it out! So here is what we will do," says the smartest man. "Since I'm the smartest, I will climb up the tree first, and then I will climb onto the sturdiest branch. I will grab a hold of the branch and hang down from my hands. Then another one of you will follow me. He will then grab a hold of my legs and hang down from them! We will then continue this action one after the other. Very soon, we will become so heavy that the tree will break from the weight of the pressure!"

"Excellent idea! That is why you are called the smartest man!" exclaimed the settlers.

The settlers started to execute the plan. Up went the smartest one to the top and soon he was hanging from the branch, followed by another and then the next, all of whom hung from each other's feet. After a while, they were all hanging there, and their plan was indeed a working plan! The tree soon began to bend, and swing, giving off noises of weakening under the pressure. They all agreed their plan was working, and soon they would be able to get all the logs for their new house!

However, the smartest man at the top was beginning to feel the pressure even more than the tree itself. The weight became so heavy, too heavy for him. Under great strain and pressure, he encouraged the others to be as heavy as they could, while he took a better grip, and moistened his hand with some spit. Having let go of his grip to moisten his hand, they all fell like a deck of cards and lay in a pile on the ground.

Then it suddenly occurred to everyone that their plan had failed. Not people to be easily discouraged, they started to think what to do next. People of Finland strongly believe that the task at hand must have been a terrible mental stress to the settlers to have to brainstorm so much. However, they were up for the task and started to brainstorm once again. Once more, the smartest one spoke, "I've a plan!"

"Please tell us! You know you are the smartest one!"

"Since we cannot break the trees, then we will have to burn the trees down!"

"Yes, we all agree. We trust you since you are the smartest one!"

The smartest one reached for the Bemböle's only box of matches and took out one match. Just then he had a second thought, what if this match didn't work? So he decided to try the match out first. He took the match and made contact with the side of the box. Without any hesitation, the match was ablaze.

"Oh yes, it does work!" He puffed at the match, and it went out, and in this way, the smartest one continued to test the other matches just in case the other matches didn't work. He repeated the behaviour several times until he had tested all the matches in the box. Feeling pleased with himself, the smartest one shouted out, "What a relief knowing that all the matches do work! Time for action! Let us light up that tree and get some lumber," as he smiled feeling very accomplished and pleased with himself.

"You know, men, I had a strange experience which made me start thinking. When I fell down from the tree we were trying to break and landed on the ground, I saw stars and sparks. I got to thinking that if I repeat the experience by you hitting me, we could catch some of the sparks and use it to set the tree ablaze. That I think is one of the smartest ideas we have come up with."

Everyone agreed and asked the smart man just how he intended to put this plan into action.

"All of you will hit me until I can see sparks and stars, once again. At that moment, I'll call out to you, and you'll catch the sparks to light up the tree, okay?"

All the Settlers agreed and were ready as soon as the smart one gave the signal. All the Bemböle men converged on the poor smart man. They spared the smart one no pains as they all applied blow after blow. Well needless to say, he saw a lot of stars and sparks, but somehow they were not able to set a tree ablaze with it.

Unable to bear the pain any longer, the smart man yelled, "Stop! Stop! I think I finally get it!" It was as if a new vision had come to him.

"Let us go and find our axes, and start cutting down the trees!"

"Yes, of course, that what we will all do. You are so smart," cried the settlers.

So they fetched their axes and got to work. Together, they could harvest as many good and straight trees as they needed – enough to build a strong new log house.

I am not sure you want to know what happened next! That, my friend, is another story!

THE MAGIC ORANGE TREE

A folktale from Haiti: Retold.

This legend is about an unfortunate little girl who lost her mother at birth. It took her father a long time after her mother died to considering remarrying. However, when he did commit to doing so, he married a woman who would turn out to be both mean and cruel. In her stepmother meanness, she would often let the little girl go hungry by denying her food to eat. Of course, the girl would often be very hungry.

To the delight of the young girl, she came from school one day and found three round ripe oranges on the table. She took a deep breath, savouring the smell of the fruit. The smell filled her senses making her mouth water. Next, she looked around to see where her stepmother was. No one was in sight. Unable to resist the temptation, she stole one orange, peeled it, and ate it savouring every segment. She licked the juices around her lips, and they felt like more. It was soooo good.

Yielding to temptation, she took a second orange and devoured it. After eating the second orange, the girl decided that since she was now guilty of stealing two of the oranges, she might as well have the third one. She was not quite so hungry at this point, so she ate it slowly and enjoyed every single drop of juice from this third orange. Ohhh my, she was so delighted. However, her happiness would be short-lived since her step-mom soon came home.

The stepmother yelled, "Who took the three oranges I left on the table? Whoever has taken those oranges had better say their prayers now, and give God their souls because their behind belongs to me! However, they will never again be able to pray!"

The terrified young girl ran from the house to seek some sort of refuge. She hurried through the woods and ran until she came to her own mother's resting place. As she sat there, she cried and prayed to her mother all night to help her. Exhausted, she finally she fell asleep.

The sun was bright and as she woke up in the morning. As she stood up, something fell from her lap onto the ground. She frantically looked around to see what it might be. What was it? It was a seed from an orange. To her astonishment, the moment, it hit the earth something magical happened. A green leaf sprouted from a young shoot. With a mixture of emotions, the girl watched in amazement. Then she knelt down and began to encourage the plant as she sang:

"My orange tree, please grow and grow and grow. Orange tree, orange tree, please grow and grow and grow for me," and she began to talk to the little tree.

"Orange tree, please grow for you know my Stepmother is not my real mother. Please, my orange tree."

Sure enough, the obedient little orange tree grew. It very quickly grew to the size of the girl. The girl continued to sing and encourage the orange tree:

"Please, orange tree, show me your branches and branch and branch. Please, my orange tree, orange tree, keep branching and branching and branching, for you know orange tree, Stepmother is not my real mother, my little Orange tree."

The tree began twisting, turning, shooting branches appeared everywhere on the tree. The little girl continued to sing and encourage the tree. "Stepmother is not my real mother, my little Orange tree."

"Please, orange tree, flower and bloom, flower and bloom, Stepmother is not my real mother, my little orange tree."

"Orange tree, orange tree, bloom and bloom and bloom. Stepmother is not my real mother, my little orange tree."

Then, in obedience, the beautiful white blossoms dominated the tree. Then, after a while, the beautiful blossoms began to fade, and small green buds manifested where the flowers had once been. The girl sang:

"Please, orange tree, grow me some oranges for you know Stepmother is not my own mother, my little Orange tree."

"Oh, my orange tree, please ripen and ripen and ripen your fruit. Stepmother is not my real mother, my little orange tree."

"Please, my orange tree, orange tree, ripen and ripen and ripen, for you know too well Stepmother is not my real mother, my little orange tree."

To her surprise, as if she was dreaming, the oranges ripened, and the whole tree flourished with golden oranges. The girl was so delighted she danced around and around the tree, repeating her song:

"Please orange tree, grow me some oranges for you know Stepmother is not my real mother, my little orange tree."

"Oh, my orange tree, please ripen and ripen and ripen your fruit. Stepmother is not my real mother, my little orange tree."

"Please, my orange tree, orange tree, ripen and ripen and ripen, for you know too well Stepmother is not my real mother, my little orange tree."

To her surprise when she looked up at the tree, she saw the orange tree had grown up so tall that it was almost reaching to the sky. It was far beyond her reach.

"Oh dear, what am I going to do now?" wondered the girl.

However, the clever girl began to sing once more. She sang:

"Oh, my orange tree, please lower and lower and lower, for you know Stepmother is not my real mother, my little orange tree."

"Oh, my orange tree, please lower and lower and lower, for you know Stepmother is not my real mother, my little orange tree."

"Oh my orange tree, please lower and lower and lower, for you know Stepmother is not my real mother, my little orange tree."

The obedient orange heard the girl, and the orange tree came down to her height. In her excitement, the girl filled her arms with oranges and returned home.

The moment the stepmother caught sight of the golden oranges in the little girl's arms, she grabbed them and began to eat them. Soon she had eaten all the oranges. Then, she finally spoke to the little girl, "Tell me, my child, where have you found such delicious oranges?"

The frightened girl did not want to say. The stepmother tightened her mean grip on the girl's wrist and began to twist it. The mean woman ordered the girl "Tell me, where did you find those oranges?"

The terrified girl led her stepmother through the woods to the orange tree. The clever girl began to sing as soon as she came to the tree. She sang:

"Please, orange tree, grow me some oranges for you know Stepmother is not my real mother, my little orange tree. Stepmother is not my real mother, my dear orange tree."

And the orange tree grew up to the sky. The stepmother did not know what to make of this, since she was very frightened. She began to plead and beg the little girl to make the tree stop.

"Please, my child; you will always be my own dear child. You can always have as much as you want to eat, and I will make sure you are never hungry. Please, tell the tree to come down so you can pick the oranges for me."

So the girl quietly sang:

"Oh, my orange tree, please lower and lower and lower, for you know Stepmother is not my real mother, my little orange tree."

"Oh, my orange tree, please lower and lower and lower, for you know Stepmother is not my real mother, my little orange tree."

"Oh, my orange tree, please lower and lower and lower, for you know Stepmother is not my real mother, my little orange tree."

The tree started to lower. When the tree had lowered itself to the height of the stepmother, she quickly leaped on to the tree and began to mount the tree so

quickly that she seemed to be climbing as fast as any monkey would. She swung from branch to branch. She greedily ate every orange. The girl saw that there would soon be no oranges left. Then, in an act of revenge the little girl sang:

"Please, orange tree, grow me some oranges for you know Stepmother is not my real mother, my little orange tree. Stepmother is not my real mother, my dear orange tree."

And the orange tree grew up to the sky. The stepmother did not know what to make of this, since she was very frightened. She began to plead and beg the little girl to make the tree stop.

"Please, help me, my child!" cried the stepmother as she rose into the sky. Her voice was becoming fainter as the tree grew taller. "Help me. Please! Help me, please! Help me, please!"

Then the vengeful girl cried: "Break! Orange tree, Break!"

The orange tree snapped into a thousand pieces.

The little girl searched among the branches until she found a tiny orange seed. She gently placed it in the ground and planted it in the earth as she sang softly:

"Please, orange tree, grow and grow and grow. Please, orange tree, grow and grow and grow just for me. Stepmother is not real my mother, orange tree."

The orange tree happily obliges and grew to the height of the girl. This height allowed her to pick some oranges and sell them at the market. They were such sweet oranges that the girl was sold out in no time at all.

And so every single Saturday she took her oranges to market and sold them.

THE LEGEND OF THE SPARROW

This is a Chinese Buddhist children's story Retold.

Taiwan: Even in a weak and poorly state as Mrs Fan lay on her bed, she did not want anyone to worry about her, so she kept reassuring them that she would get better slowly but surely and that they were not to worry about her.

Mrs. Fan reassured her husband as she lay in bed, even though she had been very ill for months. Her caring husband, Mr Fan, took her hand in his and comforted her in reaction to her concerns. "You're my wife. How can I not want to see you get better? I must think of a way to help you become well again. I still hope that we can share in the birth of a son."

"Cough, cough, cough!"Mrs. Fan could not stop coughing.

Just then her husband had an announcement for her. "I think your illness is getting worse. I am very concerned about you and I want you to get better." So Mr.Fan explained to his wife that yesterday he had been to see the Daoist Fang and explained to him her illness. "In return, he gave me a prescription which I would like you to at least give a try. So, what do you say, we try it?"

Not waiting for his wife approval Mr. Fan stood up and went to fetch the prescription.

Mrs. Fan retorted, "What prescription?"

Clearing his throat, Mr Fan hesitated for a bit then explained that the prescription states that we need to keep 100 sparrows and we need to feed them herb-infused rice. After 21 days, we will slaughter them and consume their brains."

Mrs. Fan was shocked and retorted, "What? You expect me to eat the brains of 100 sparrows? No! No! No! No way! This is far too savage an act. It is a selfish act, and I cannot condone such a cruel act." Steadily shaking her head, in utter displeasure, she refused the prescription.

Then Mr Fan implored with his wife, "Whether it is savage or not savage, I want you to get well again, and you must do whatever it takes to make yourself better. Furthermore, Daoist Fang assured me that this prescription is very effective for your condition."

Mr. Fan took no heed of his wife's disapproval. Determined, he went downtown and bought 100 fat sparrows and brought them home. He held them in a cage and then he went to the Chinese herbalist to purchase the herb-infused rice. As Mrs. Fan lay silently in her bed, she could hear the twittering of the sparrows. She knew that her husband was determined to put his plan into action. She could not help feeling disgusted over the whole issue as Mrs. Fan pondered what she should do.

Then as she lay in her bed, she reasoned, "Normally, I could not even be hard-hearted enough to carelessly step on an ant. Now we're going to slay 100 beautiful sparrows just to save one life. How could I have the heart to do such a cruel thing? Kill 100 lives to maybe save one life? This makes no sense to me!"

Mrs. Fan cared enough that she started thinking of just how she could spare the lives of these birds. With strong determination, she got the courage to walk and creep slowly to the courtyard. Once she got there, she unlocked the sparrows' cage and granted 100 sparrows their God-given right to freedom. When Mr Fan returned home with the herb-infused rice, he saw the empty cage. Mr Fan knew instantly that his wife had set the birds free because she was not prepared to consume them, so he had no choice but to let the issue drop.

Stranger still was the turn in Mrs Fan's health and wellness. After she had set free the 100 sparrows, her mental state became strangely calm and relaxed. She began to recover slowly and gradually. Even stranger still, one year later Mrs Fan gave birth to a baby boy. Mr. Fan was giddy as a child as he held his new son; he could not help laughing as he clung to his child, showing him to his wife.

"See my dear, our son is so perfect and lovely!"

However, to their surprise, at the very moment both parents noticed that under the baby's arms were many black spots. Upon examination, they observed that the shapes of the spots strongly resembled the shapes of the sparrows and there were exactly 100 spots.

If this legend is true, what do you think of this strange phenomenon?

A MOHAWK LEGEND OF THE FLUTE

A folktale from Canada. Retold.

The boy's way of welcoming a brand new day was to take his flute and head for the lake to serenade the morning as his eyes beheld the sun gently warming the forest floor with its warm strokes of love. He heard the call of the elk and in his mind it sounded like a good morning call from nature itself. The elk was also serenading the sunrise of the splendour of a superb morning. The boy thought, "Like me, it is his way of welcoming the new day." He sat on the shores of the lake facing east, first, offering gratitude to the Creator and then with his flute, he welcomed the day with a gift of a song. Soon he was greeted by some more friends of nature, three loons, as they communicated with song.

As they sat on the shores of the lake, the loon enquired of the boy, "Do you have any idea where and how the voice of flute came about?"

"I must admit I do not know."

The loon then volunteered to tell the boy. "A very long time ago our ancestors were once a part of the Anishenabeg people. Among them was a very caring young girl who was the daughter of the chief. Her name was Tiobi. She loved the loon and had a special bond with them. Tiobi cared very much for the loons and would come down to the lake every day to welcome them at the lake. This special bond was built on mutual respect; she respected them and likewise, the loons respected and trusted her. Tiobi cared so much for the loons that she managed to convince her tribe not to hunt the loon; Tiobi managed to convince her people that the loons were a sacred bird. She explained to them that the loons cry because they are trying to say that they are misplaced and the Anishenabeg people should help them.

Tiobi got up one morning and took to the shores of the lake to rescue a loon in the lake. She took her canoe and paddled out to the center of the lake. As she reached towards the lost loon in the water, she reassured him, "Don't you worry my little loon, I will make certain you find your way."As Tiobi tried to reach the loon, the canoe tipped over and she fell into the water and drowned. Tiobi's father was most sad for the death of his beloved daughter. The following morning a loon called out from the lake. However, the chief was so caught up in his grief that he did not hear the cry of the lonely loon.

The loon called to elk for a helping hand. "My dear Elk, could you please croon your morning song?" The elk was happy to oblige and he sang an enchanting song and sure enough the chief woke to the song. He hurried down to the lake to see the elk that had been singing. However, there were none to be found. In its place, he saw a loon gazing up at him.

"My little Loon, I can see white spots on your back. Are these tears?" whispered the chief. "Are you disorientated? Have you lost your way, little bird?" Then all of a sudden the Chief realised he felt a connection to the loon and sensed that he was in the company of his daughter. Instantly, he acknowledged her presence and wept as he asked, "My daughter, is it you who has come to comfort me?" He felt very happy within his spirit and yet at the same time he also felt broken-hearted. The Chief tried desperately to understand what his daughter, the loon, was trying to say.

Not knowing what else to do he ran into the woods and pleaded with the Great Spirit. "Great Spirit, please, can you help me understand what my daughter, the loon, is trying to tell me. Help me to be able to communicate with her, so she can understand me and me her!" Just then the lighting flashed and a branch fell where a woodpecker had been working on it. The chief picked it up and upon examining the branch he saw that it had a shallow hole inside at both ends. To test the hole, he blew into the wood at one end of the stick and out of it came a beautiful sound, just like the loon.

The chief took his stick and hurried back. He blew into the stick in an effort to communicate with his daughter. Then, he played a song in which he said, "My beloved daughter, the Great Spirit has given me a gift that I can use to communicate with you. This gift is called a flute, and I will use it to serenade you in song like the elk did not so long ago, and through this flute you will hear my the song of my heart and I will hear yours. I understand that you,are lost on your journey and also all those of my Anishenabeg people who have died by drowning.

"You have now joined the tribe of the 'Loons' and cry because you are also sad. I now understand that we, your people, do not hear your cry; I can now see the tears have been manifest on your back as a reminder to your people. With this gift from the Great Spirit, I will sing a song of prayer for you, and you will find your way to the assembly table and sit among our people who will be there to welcome you." The chief played blissfully from his heart and the loons disappeared.

And so it is said that every year the loon reappeared and the chief understood these loons were tragedies of his people who abide among the lakes.